A TALE OF DESIRE – VOLUME ONE

BY
JD NELSON

To Nels, always Nels

CHAPTER ONE

I was leaning against the side of my building in my brand-new lingerie, smoking my second joint of the day, when a blue-eyed, blond-haired Viking showed up. I watched him as he carefully parked in front of the hardware store next door and tried to unfold his long legs from a vintage Chevrolet truck without it being too obvious that he needed a much more substantial vehicle to accommodate his tall frame.

"Excuse me," he called when he straightened, motioning to the beige wall behind my back. "Do you know how to get into that building?"

I studied the man's ruggedly handsome face, took another drag, then stubbed the joint out. "Depends. You here to rob the place, or are you here as a potential client?"

He flashed a small irritated smile as he gave me a once-over. "Look, I'm not here for sex."

"And I'm not offering it with an attitude like that," I grumbled, turning on my heel and heading back toward the entrance. "Jerk."

"Wait! Is that the way in?" he asked.

I didn't bother to turn around. "Like I said, not with that attitude."

"Hey!" the Viking shouted again, jogging toward me.

He laid a hand on my shoulder when he got close, and without thinking, I threw my right hand up, grabbed his wrist, and twisted his arm sharply, putting my left hand at the back of his elbow. I gave his elbow a little pressure, making the handsome man grunt in pain. "Don't touch me, okay?"

"Okay!" he cried, yanking out of my grip the moment I eased up. "I wasn't going to hurt you. I just need to know how to get into this place. I'm here for a job interview."

1

"What?" I asked, starting to laugh so hard, I had to brace my hands on my knees. "Please, tell me you're kidding."

Somewhat ruffled, the Viking straightened his shirt and huffed out, "I'm not. I'm applying for the security guard position here. Though, I don't know why they need one. You seem to have things well in hand."

"Thanks," I told him, pushing my blonde hair out of my eyes and wiping tears of laughter from my cheeks. "But I'm still looking because I need someone to protect me while I can't protect myself."

His mouth dropped open. "Are you Jasmine Locke?"

"The one and only. And you are?"

"Kasper Johansson. I have a one o'clock appointment. That is if you'll still consider me after all this."

I stared into the depths of Kasper's deep blue eyes. Until this week, I had thought I'd been great at sussing out the bad guys from the good. But recent developments had me doubting my gift. He didn't appear to be the type of guy who would accost ladies in silky bedroom attire in a parking lot, but here we were. Could I trust him?

After a very long moment's reflection, I said, "I will consider you, Kasper. So long as you're able to keep your hands to yourself around me and off your dick while you're on the job."

Golden eyebrows raised, he nodded slowly. "That won't be a problem, Miss Locke. And I'm sorry. I didn't mean to hurt or scare you."

"Hurt me?" I scoffed. "I kind of kicked your ass."

He chuckled. "Should I even bother coming in, then?"

I sized him up. Kasper Johansson was huge, but not so muscled up he couldn't be quick when he needed to be. And he was tall, maybe six-three or four. His hands made nearly three of mine. I nodded when I was done with my cursory examination and opened the door for him. "You look like a man who can handle his own. I just need to know if you can handle the job."

Kasper followed me to the large office I'd turned into my sanctuary, handed me his resume, and sat in the plush purple chair in front of my desk. "I've had several security jobs since I was discharged from the Army. I'm sure I can handle whatever the job entails."

After tossing the blue folder to the side of my desk, I powered up my iPad. "I don't doubt your skills, Kasper. I just need to know I can trust you to keep your mind on your job while I'm doing mine."

His forehead furrowed. "What is your job?"

I tapped the iPad and spun it around so that he could see the screen. "I fuck rich men for money."

Kasper's eyes widened as my words and what he saw sank in. "You have sex? Here? In this old office building?"

"Yes." I pursed my lips when he seemed too stunned to respond, then continued, leaving the video on to gauge his reaction. "Most of my clients are long-term clients, but I have to take on a new one now and then to … uh, replenish the stock. Those are the ones I'm most concerned about. I had a bad experience recently. I don't want a repeat of that … ever."

"Bad experience?" he asked, shifting uncomfortably in his chair. "What kind of bad experience?"

"See for yourself," I told him, selecting the video I'd prepared for the interview. I handed him the iPad. "The right side is the camera inside of the room next door. The left is the camera in the security booth that looks into that room through a two-way mirror."

Taking a deep breath, he nodded. "Okay."

I watched his face as he hit play, not knowing how to feel. I was a prostitute, sure, but I was still embarrassed to have hardcore sex in front of such a handsome stranger.

As the sounds of me begging for cock filled the room, Kasper shifted in his seat. "I apologize," he said, lowering the iPad to partially cover himself. "Miss Locke, I can assure you my self-control will not be an issue if I get this job."

3

Of their own volition, my eyes drifted to his impressive erection. I wasn't mad about it, not in the least. How could I be? I was essentially making him watch porn. Not to mention, seeing him get turned on by me was damn flattering to the ego.

I moistened my mouth before I spoke. "It's okay. I'll take it as a compliment. But, Kasper, you'll have to numb yourself to it. You can't be hindered by an erection while I'm with a client. You'll see why in a minute."

He gasped as the moment I'd referred to flashed before his eyes. Of course, I knew exactly what he would see. I'd watched both videos a hundred times over the past few days. I could still feel the rough hands around my neck and the lightness in my head as I came close to blacking out. It only lasted a few seconds; the new client came right after, but it was enough to make me fire John before I even had a chance to peruse what turned out to be a very incriminating video of his actions in the security office.

"What the fuck is he doing?" Kasper demanded, pointing at John, who had pulled his dick out and started to jack off instead of intervening. "That asshole!"

"Yeah, I told him as much when I had him escorted off the property. That's why you're here, Mr. Johansson. I need someone who's willing to focus more on his job than his dick. Do you think you can do that?"

His jaw clenched and he shook his head in disgust as he watched the client slip into the security office. My long-time guard never even slowed the speed of his strokes as he watched me get dressed. Nor did he stop when he thanked the client for giving it to me the way he would if I would deign to fuck him.

When the clip finally ended, Kasper met my eyes. "If you hire me, this will never happen to you again."

"Then, Kasper Johansson, you're hired. I only work a few days out of the week, so you'll be paid daily. How does eight hundred a day, plus health and dental benefits sound?"

His eyes went wide. "Eight hundred a day?"

4

I shrugged. "I make a pretty penny off the clients and own the building. I can afford it. Plus, you're not going to be working forty hours a week. I want you to be able to make ends meet. I don't want to have to compete with another job for your time."

"That sounds ... more than fair."

I handed him a packet with all of his insurance information and the charger for the iPad. "I want you to take this iPad home and do a little homework to prepare for your first week. Is that okay?"

His eyes met mine. "Homework?"

"It has some of my clients on it," I explained, leaning over the desk to show him the thumbnails, accidentally making one play. "I want you to watch these, so you'll know what to expect and become accustomed to seeing me ... you know."

He grinned as he saw me walk into a room fully dressed in a black leather bondage outfit. "You're sending me home with porn?"

"That's exactly what I'm doing, Kasper. Watch the videos tonight. I'll call you sometime tomorrow afternoon. We'll go over everything else. You'll start on Thursday morning at ten."

He paused the video and stood to shake my hand over the desk. "Thank you, Miss Locke. I won't disappoint you."

Smiling, I took his hand. I had to admire his tenacity. This meeting was probably the most awkward job interview anyone had ever had.

"Jasmine," I said, completely mortified when my eyes wandered south. "Just call me Jasmine."

He gave me a crooked grin as he straightened. "I look forward to your call, Jasmine."

"I ... uh ... Oh, just get that thing out of here," I said, waving his penis away. "I can't think when it's staring me in the face."

He snickered as he walked to the door. "Sorry, boss."

Embarrassed, I buried my red face in my hands. "Not half as sorry as I am."

CHAPTER TWO

At eleven o'clock the next morning, I drove to the office with every intention of finishing the invoices for the clients I'd scheduled during the week. I'd been so embarrassed by my inability to keep my eyes from Kasper's crotch yesterday, I'd left the office almost as quickly as he did. But as soon as I unlocked the door, I found myself way too curious to get straight to work. I wanted to know more about the smoking hot man who would be seeing me in a plethora of compromising positions for the foreseeable future.

Making a beeline for my desk after I locked the door behind me, I picked up the blue folder he'd left with me and leaned back in my chair to peruse Mr. Kasper Håkan Johansson's resume and background check for anything that might stand out. I found nothing. Everything he told me had checked out satisfactorily. More than satisfactory, actually. He seemed to be a model citizen. That was a massive step in the right direction for me. The guy who had his position before had been an ex-con with a penchant for lying and the occasional prostitute and/or good time.

With my hopes high, I picked up my cell and dialed Kasper's number, hoping like hell he hadn't changed his mind overnight.

The sound of my heavy breathing was the first thing I heard when he picked up, immediately followed by his gruff voice. "Hello?" he asked.

"Hi, Kasper. It's Jasmine Locke."

"Hi, Jasmine. Give me a sec." He fumbled with the phone, and I heard my breathing stop. "How are you today?"

I pressed my lips together to keep from laughing. "I'm good. How's it going over there?"

He chuckled. "Honestly?"

"That's the best policy," I replied brightly.

"I don't know how you do this for a living. These men are ..." He trailed off, lost for words, then sighed. "I guess it's that they're just so ... all over you."

"Well, that is what they pay me for."

"Yeah, but do you like being used like this?" he asked, sounding genuinely concerned.

I shrugged, though he couldn't see me. I'd been asked this question many times before. "I don't *not* like it," I told him. "If you'll notice, I'm enjoying myself quite a bit."

He chuckled again. "I noticed."

"I mean, sure, some of them are senior citizens, but I still enjoy them. Cialis works wonders, you know."

"That it does." He paused for a second before continuing. "So, are you calling to see if I'm doing my homework, or is there something else you'd like to talk about?"

"Both. I was wondering if you would like to have lunch with me. I could give you a rundown of the selection procedure and answer any questions you might have before your first day."

"Sounds like a plan. Where did you have in mind?"

I tapped my chin. "What about the Mexican place on Mountain City Highway? A margarita sounds pretty good right now."

"Sounds good. After the last couple of hours of 'homework,' I could go for a beer and a burrito. Meet you there in twenty minutes?"

"Perfect. See you then."

"Yes, you will."

I hung up the phone and leaned back in my chair. Kasper was so different than anyone I'd interviewed before. Most of the applicants had made lewd comments to me after being shown the video, and a few had even gotten up and walked out the door after finding out what the job entailed. Kasper wasn't anything like those men. Hell, he wasn't like any man I'd met before in my life. Not only had he appeared to be protective of me almost immediately after meeting me, but he also seemed to find the whole thing ultra-amusing, and as weird as that sounded, it soothed me a bit.

***

Kasper was already waiting at the bar, wearing a broad smile and deliciously tight blue jeans, when I arrived. He waved me over and pulled out a chair for me.

"I took the liberty of ordering you one of their specials," he said, gesturing to an electric blue drink in a margarita glass. "I'm told it's delightfully different."

I raised an eyebrow at his presumption.

"Guess I should've waited, huh?" he asked, cringing under my glare.

"No," I assured him. "It's fine. As long as you don't mind me ordering for you." I leaned over the bar to ask for my two favorite plates, then sat down next to him.

"Touché," he said, laughing. "What do I get?"

"Grilled chicken and steak in a spicy sauce."

"Nicely done. That sounds good." He held up his drink. "To overstepping boundaries?"

I clinked my glass against his bottle of beer. "To overstepping boundaries."

"Mind if I cross one more?" he asked.

Intrigued, I moved my bar stool closer. "Not a bit."

"Good. Because I have got to tell you, Jasmine, I've masturbated more times in the last twenty-four hours than I have in the past year."

I choked on the mouthful of margarita I'd just sipped and laughed. "I think that's probably for the best. Get it all out of your system now, you know?"

"I'm trying, but I'm not sure I can. I'm fighting like hell not to get an erection right now." He grimaced when he realized how that

8

must sound, and added, "You have nothing to worry about, of course. I can control myself."

"Then I am both appreciative and disappointed," I purred, leaning a little closer to him. "I haven't stopped thinking about your not even close to little problem since yesterday."

"Fuck me," he muttered before taking a long swig of his beer.

"Is that a request?" I asked.

He blew out a breath. "I can't tell if you're being serious or not, but either way, I think I need several more drinks."

"Drinks? No, we need shots."

His brows shot up. "At lunch?"

I shrugged. "Why not? We're celebrating. Do you have somewhere you need to be today?"

He threw up his hands in surrender. "What the hell? What kind of shots are we talking about?"

I rolled my eyes in mock exaggeration. "Duh, tequila. Tequila is the only acceptable shot to take in a Mexican restaurant ... or really, ever."

Chuckling, he motioned to the bartender. "A bottle of your finest tequila, lime, and salt, please."

With a nod, the bartender dipped underneath the counter and reappeared with a white-labeled bottle and two shot glasses. "Will this do?"

"Perfect," Kasper said. Turning to me, he asked, "Want to play Truth or Drink?"

"Truth or Drink?" I asked. "That sounds a little ominous."

He waggled his hand. "Eh, it could be. It's fifty-fifty in my experience. Sometimes, it's fun. Sometimes, it's far too revealing and traumatizing. It really could go either way."

I grinned as the bartender sat down a small whiskey glass full of sliced limes and several packets of salt. "You're on."

Kasper twisted the top off the tequila and poured two shots. "Okay," he said, handing me a glass. "Truth or Drink?"

"Truth."

Sitting back in his chair, he looked me over, his eyes settling on my ring finger. "Do you have a boyfriend or husband?"

"Do you honestly think I'd be discussing your hard dick with you if I did?"

"No! I mean … look, I didn't mean to imply anything, Jasmine."

I couldn't help but laugh at his discomfort. "You're pretty flustered right now, aren't you?"

He ran a hand through his blond hair and nodded. "I like to think of myself as a rational person, one who wouldn't fuck you right here on this bar, but you are definitely pushing all my limits. You make me very nervous … in the best sense."

"Well, I do know a thing or two about pushing and limits," I said cheekily. "I hear I'm pretty good at it."

Groaning, he closed his eyes. "See, that kind of thing is the reason I'm going to need a cold shower after lunch."

"Don't feel bad," I told him, "you're not alone. All this talk about your cock … I might have to make use of my favorite vibrator and your résumé photo."

He swallowed hard and tipped his beer in my direction for a toast. "To masturbating at home and not at work?"

"I'm literally required to masturbate at work, but yeah, to masturbating at home."

He clinked his bottle against my glass and shook his head. "This has been the weirdest two days of my life."

"I do tend to have that effect on people."

"But not on anyone special?"

I sighed. "Not for a while, actually. I dated a guy pretty seriously a few years ago, but just like the others before him, he couldn't deal with my job." I shrugged. "He said it made him feel inadequate."

He nodded. "I guess a guy would need a pretty healthy ego to be with you, huh?"

I threw back the shot, though I didn't have to. I was going to need a drink or three to talk about my personal life ... or lack thereof. "Honestly, Kasper, I'm not sure that guy exists. Inadequacy aside, I want a real relationship out of the guys I date. But that doesn't seem to be what they want."

His forehead furrowed as he tried to work out what I meant. "I don't understand."

"All of the guys I've dated since I've started this job have felt like they could go out and sleep with other women because I sleep with other men. I can't put up with that. I'm a one man at a time kind of woman." Shaking my head, I chuckled to myself. "I know that must sound crazy."

Kasper smiled and put his hand on top of mine. "It doesn't sound crazy at all. You want stability and faithfulness. There's nothing wrong with that. Your job is just that—your job. It has nothing to do with your personal life."

"Could you maybe explain that to my exes?" I asked, holding my shot glass out for a refill. "They didn't understand it when I told them."

He gave me a bitter smile. "Those kinds of guys, they don't deserve someone like you. You're great. If they can't see that and don't want to have a monogamous relationship with you, you're better off without them."

"How do you know I'm so great?" I asked, acutely aware of the big, warm hand still covering my own.

"I'm an excellent judge of character. I can usually read a person the second I meet them."

"Truth or Drink?" I asked suddenly. I wanted to know … no, I needed to know what he thought of me. Our acquaintanceship hadn't exactly started smoothly.

Kasper squinted at me, apparently knowing exactly what question I would ask him. He finally sighed and said, "Truth."

"What did you 'read' in me the first time we met?"

He glanced down for a second and rubbed the back of his neck, looking distinctly uncomfortable with his thoughts. "I think I'll drink instead," he said, finally moving his hand from mine to grab his shot glass. "It's probably the safest course of action."

My mouth fell open. "You thought something negative, didn't you?"

He sighed and threw back his shot without a chaser. "No," he admitted. "Definitely not. Do you realize what you were wearing? Because I am *never* going to forget what your breasts looked like in that negligee."

I sat up straight. "Tits aside, you must have thought something negative. You told me you didn't want to fuck you before I even offered."

"Did you just say, 'tits aside'?" he asked, barking out a laugh.

"Just answer the question." I shoved him on the arm.

"I think I see our food coming," he said, making a show of looking behind me.

"Nice change of subject," I whispered as the waitress set our food in front of us.

"Thank God for small miracles," he whispered back.

CHAPTER THREE

"Earth to Jasmine," he said, snapping his fingers in front of my focused eyes. "Are you still with me?"

"Yeah, I'm sorry. I ..." I trailed off as I watched him lick the web of skin between his thumb and forefinger to sprinkle salt. I couldn't stop myself from imagining what that smooth pink tongue would feel like between my legs. And those big hands! What would they feel like on my body? I wanted to know more than I wanted my next breath.

Kasper laughed. "You just can't help yourself, can you?"

Chagrined, I jerked my gaze from his left hand and shrugged. "I'm trying?"

His smile was wicked as he poured another shot and pushed the tray of lime over to me. "Last one, I think. We're going to have to Uber home as it is."

I huffed. "Wuss."

He shook his head, amused at my sassiness. "Okay, then, Miss Locke. Truth or Drink?"

"Truth," I answered, daring to meet his gaze.

"What's going on behind that pretty face and those gorgeous green eyes?" he asked. "What were you thinking just now?"

"Trust me, Kasper. You don't want to know."

He raised a brow in interest. "Don't I?"

"Nope. Definitely not."

"Come on, Jasmine. You're breaking the rules here."

"That's because I'm a rebel."

His expression didn't change.

"Okay, okay. The truth is, I can't stop thinking about your tongue. Watching you lick your hand is making me wish you *would* fuck me on this bar."

The corner of his mouth quirked up. "You're drunk."

I held up two fingers, showing him just a little bit. We had taken several shots while we ate, and I was just this side of smashed.

"Hey, man," he called to the bartender. "Can I get the check?"

The bartender nodded. "Sure thing."

Turning back to me, he pulled his credit card out of his phone case and said, "I think it's time I got you home."

I nodded, stumbling as I slid off the stool. "I think you're right."

He stood quickly and straightened me up, keeping a light hand on my waist. "Whoa, there."

"You smell nice," I told him, leaning my face against the wide expanse of his chest and breathing in deep. "Like a man."

Laughing again, he cupped my chin. "You're really cute when your defenses are down."

"Who said they're down?" I retorted. "I could still kick your ass."

He leaned over to sign the receipt with his free hand. "Sorry. I temporarily forgot what a badass you are. I apologize."

"Damn straight," I slurred. "Did you order the car?"

"I ordered it when you started swaying in your seat. Do you have everything?"

I swayed as I checked my pockets and giggled when he had to catch me from falling. "Yep."

"All right, drunkie. Let's get you out of here."

"Hey! That's ... accurate."

Laughing, he looped an arm around my shoulders as we walked out into the warm sunlight together.

14

Once we were outside, I marveled at his height. "You know, you're very tall, Kasper."

"Ever think you might be very short?" he countered, putting his hands under my arms to keep me upright.

I looked down. "Your junk is nearly at boob level. That makes you tall. And five-three isn't short. It's almost average for a woman."

"Touché, cupcake."

I squinted up at him. "What do you mean by 'cupcake'?"

He grinned down at me as the Uber driver pulled into the parking lot. "You're small, sweet, and fucking delicious."

***

When I finally woke late the next morning, I didn't remember the taxi ride home. I wasn't even sure how Kasper had figured out my address to find the house. The last thing I remembered was him calling me delicious, ushering my way past drunk self into a silver Honda, and climbing in after me.

I rolled over and looked up at the ceiling fan, sighing when I saw how dusty it was. Had Kasper seen that when he, no doubt, carried me to bed? How embarrassing. But then again, he was probably too preoccupied with my gigantic teddy bear collection to pay any attention to the fan.

"Ugh," I groaned, getting to my feet, before noticing the note on my nightstand.

I had to look through your purse to get your address. Sorry.

-Kasper

P.S. Nice teddy bears

P.P.S You kicked your shoes off somewhere between the front door and the hallway.

"Double ugh," I said, knowing I was going to have to call him with an apology at some point. Otherwise, I'd never be able to face him at work the next day. I flopped back down on the bed face first. "I'm never drinking again."

***

The next day, Kasper arrived promptly at ten in the morning, two coffees in hand. "Hey, boss!" he said, handing me a cup. "How was your day yesterday? I would've called when you texted me, but I wasn't sure how hungover you were."

I smiled while inwardly thanking God that he wasn't looking at me like I was some kind of lush. "It was fine, and I was fine, though I could've used this coffee then."

He laughed and said, "I'll bet," before he clapped his hands together and rubbed them excitedly. "So, what's first on the agenda today?"

"Well, I have to make up the rooms for my clients this week. You don't have to help with that if you don't want to. I thought you might want to check out where you'd be working. Today's client doesn't get here until twelve o'clock."

He put his coffee cup down on the table in the lobby. "That's plenty of time to do both. Lead the way."

I grinned at his enthusiasm. "Thanks! I really appreciate it. My last guy never offered to help me do this part of the job."

"It's my pleasure, boss."

"Jasmine," I corrected.

"Sorry, Jasmine."

Still grinning, I led him down the hall to the vast room I used as a storage closet and showed him around. "I keep all of the room décor and props in here," I told him. "The clients on Saturday and Sunday don't have much of a preference, other than it is modern and clean, but Mr. Evans, the twelve o'clock, he has a fondness for a traditional sex room. Black satin sheets, red leather pillows—that sort of thing."

"How does he like you dressed?"

"Today, he likes me in a tight leather corset that leaves my breasts free and four-inch heels. No panties."

Kasper was stunned silent.

"Are you going to be okay over there?"

"Yeah, just give me a minute to stop thinking about you in that getup."

"No need to think about it. You'll be seeing the real thing soon. It's going to take me an hour just to remember how to walk in those ridiculous shoes."

Laughing, he took the big box labeled 'Mr. Evans' off the shelf. "Let's go sexy it up, then."

"After you," I said, quickly grabbing my outfit de jour. "It goes in room number three."

As I walked down the hall behind Kasper, I noticed he didn't make a big show of checking things out. He was apparently trying to play it cool. But once he was inside of the room, his steps faltered as he took in the dark walls and gothic-style style bed. I, for one, thoroughly understood his hesitance. It could be a bit jarring. After all, it was primarily a sex dungeon.

"Um … are those whips?" Kasper asked, setting the box down on the nightstand.

I followed his eyes over to the far wall where twenty or so different sex implements hung. "There's nothing crazy over there, but yes, there are whips. A few of my clients like that sort of thing during sex. I have to be prepared to give them what they want when they want it."

He pulled out a black bottom sheet and threw a corner to me. "What about what you want?"

"It's irrelevant," I said, putting the sheet in place. "Although it has happened before, guys don't usually pay me a ton of money to do the things I like. They pay me for their fantasy, what makes them get off."

He tucked in the sheet at the head of the bed with a confused face. "How do you know what gets them off?"

"They fill out a questionnaire with their application."

He stared at me. "Are you serious?"

"Of course," I said, not bothering to look up. "I need repeat customers. I'll do anything within reason to keep them coming back."

"And that works?"

I stopped straightening the sheet and met his gaze. "Kasper, once you get a man off in that particular way he likes, he will never stop coming back. Who else are they going to get to do that for them?"

"So, none of these guys are married?"

"I have a policy against married clients. Unless their wives are physically unable to have sex with them and are in agreement, I won't fuck them. I'm not breaking up happy homes just because some guy wants a younger, blonder version of his wife."

His eyes widened. "You run a tight ship around here, don't you?"

"I do. And I'm aware of how rigid it all sounds, but it works for me. I do have a moral compass, you know."

He nodded, looking inexplicably mollified. "That, I can see."

CHAPTER FOUR

After we readied the rooms, I showed Kasper to the booth he'd be working from while I was indisposed. It wasn't a big room, but I felt certain it had everything I could equip it with for Kasper to keep me safe. All he would need to do was turn his comfy office chair, and he'd be able to see in all three of the "sex rooms" we'd made up. If he managed to not get distracted, my safety was as good as guaranteed.

"This is a pretty sweet setup," Kasper remarked, eyeing the monitors and controls in the booth.

"Yeah, I take my security very seriously."

"I'll say."

Smiling, I pointed at the three windows in the office. "You should be able to see everything you need to see through the two-way mirrors, but there are also numerous cameras around the rooms you can switch back and forth from using the controls or just an iPad, whichever you prefer. They'll zoom in if you think there's something you need to see up close. Trust me, I won't hate you for being overly cautious. Play around with them during Mr. Evans' time today. He's been a client for years. I don't expect anything out of him. Oh, and there's a microphone on those cameras if you think you need to call out a warning or something like that."

He pressed his lips together and nodded. "Sounds easy enough."

"Good!" I said, giving him a big smile of gratitude and a folder. "When Mr. Evans gets here, make sure he matches the picture in the portfolio and buzz him in by pressing the green button on the wall. He knows where to go." I glanced at the clock. "I need to get dressed and 'prep.' I'll see you in an about an hour and a half or so, okay?"

"Prep?" he asked, his forehead furrowed.

I bit my lip. "Well, it could mean a lot of things around here, but in this case, it means I need to masturbate. Mr. Evans likes me wet and ready for him as soon as he arrives. He's a busy man. He doesn't stay long."

Kasper stared at me, his eyes as wide as saucers. "This is the craziest job I've ever had."

"I don't doubt that for a second," I told him, opening the booth door to leave. "Have fun on your first day. And remember, don't let the clients know you're here, and please, keep it in your pants, okay?"

"That's not going to be a problem, Jasmine."

"Good. I'll see you soon."

I left Kasper in his booth and went to my quarters with my mind in disarray. I wondered what Kasper was thinking about the 'unique job opportunity' he'd accepted. Was he totally freaking out in his little security office, or was he excited by what he was about to see? My guess was he was stoically doing what his military man sense of duty told him he must, but illogically, I hoped he was anticipating seeing me fuck my client. The thought of Kasper watching me was making me wetter than I'd ever been for Mr. Evans without even touching myself.

When I was finally finished with my hair and face, I grabbed the new corset, took one look at it, and rolled my eyes. I couldn't put it on without help. "Kasper?" I called, slipping on the sky-high shoes and shutting my office door behind me. "Can you give me a hand with my corset strings, please? I don't think I thought this whole thing through."

"I'm coming," he said from inside of the security room.

"I sincerely hope not," I teased. "I thought we talked about that."

"That's not funny," he grumbled, meeting in the hallway, though his voice held a fair amount of humor.

I laughed. "It's a little funny."

"No, it's …" Kasper trailed off as he rounded the corner into the hallway. "Wow. You're really fucking naked."

"Nice of you to notice," I said, laughing again.

He scrubbed a hand over his face. "Sorry, I didn't mean to make it awkward. I just wasn't expecting all of …" He gestured to my nakedness. "All this."

"How about I give you a warning next time?"

"That would probably be for the best," he said, shooting me a relieved smile.

I chuckled, trying to keep the situation light. "Kasper, you know what you're about to witness, right? You're going to see a whole lot more of me than this."

"I know, but I think I need to take this one insane ass step at a time."

"Whatever makes you comfortable," I told him, following him into the room Mr. Evans favored.

He went straight to work as soon as we were in the room, knowing time was of the essence. "How tight do you want it?"

"Not too tight," I told him. "I like to breathe."

"No cracked ribs. Got it."

As he laced me up, I held on to the bedpost and made small talk. "So, Kasper Johansson, you've obviously done this before. Does your girlfriend wear corsets?"

"Yes and no."

I peered over my shoulder at him. "Huh?"

"No, I don't have a girlfriend. And yes, I've done this before, though not with anything as sexy as this. My cousin travels the Renaissance circuit. She dresses as a bar wench."

"Does she do it topless, too?"

He deftly tied a bow as he answered, "You know, this was kind of sexy until you asked that."

I laughed again. "Sorry. How do I look?"

Taking a step back, he gave me a naughty smile. "You look good enough to eat, cupcake."

"Yes, but do I look good enough for a sixty-year-old man to want to fuck?"

He pursed his lips as he took in the entirety of my naked state. "I can't say. I'm not sixty. However, I will say you look good enough for a thirty-one-year-old man to want to fuck. I'm going to have to ice myself down tonight."

"Good," I said primly. "That's just what a woman likes to hear."

"Is there anything else I can help you with before I go?"

"No," I replied, shooing him out. "Now, be a good boy and go watch me masturbate."

"This job is so demanding!" he griped. "First, you pay me ridiculously well. Then I have to watch a hot woman bring herself to orgasm. I don't know how much longer I can stand this."

Picking up my favorite vibrator, I shook it at him. "Very funny."

"See you soon, sexy lady." He laughed as he closed the door.

Lying back on the bed, I stared at the mirror, feeling a little self-conscious. Masturbating in front of my security guard wasn't abnormal. But with Kasper watching me, it felt different than it had felt with John. It was exciting and very, very hot.

Before I could lose my nerve, I twisted the vibrator to its lowest setting and barely slid the tip across my clit, gasping at the sensation. Groaning, I did it once more, this time holding it there longer. I looked in the mirror, again wondering what Kasper was thinking, wondering if he was hard while he watched me fuck myself with the glittery pink phallus. Those thoughts led to me think about the pink tongue I'd seen dart out to lick the delicate web between his forefinger and thumb at the bar. That prompted me to think about what that tongue would feel like if it was against my hardened clit, which drove me to think about the hard length I'd seen behind his blue jeans on his interview day. And before long, I was coming so hard, I nearly screamed out his name.

Two minutes later, I heard the buzzer on the front door. Giving Kasper two thumbs up, I waited patiently on the side of the bed for Arthur Evans to enter.

"Arthur, how nice to see you," I greeted, standing up to hug the tall, silver-haired man.

He slid his hands down the sides of my corset to cup my naked ass. "It's nice to see you, too, Jasmine. It's been too long since my last visit."

"You just saw me a week ago, you naughty man," I said, slipping my arms around his neck.

Planting a soft kiss on my lips, he growled, "If I had the time, I'd take all your appointments, sweet thing."

"And I would let you," I told him as I unzipped his dress slacks and palmed his growing erection. "I love this big cock."

He shrugged out of his jacket and loosened his tie to slip it over his head. "I think you're the naughty one today, Jasmine."

"Me?" I asked, feigning ignorance.

"Yes, you." He unbuckled his belt and slid it through the loops. "Shall I show you what I do to naughty women?"

I gave him a wide-eyed, innocent look. "Will it hurt?"

"Only a little sting," he replied, slipping out of his shoes.

"Will I like it?" I purred.

"Get on your hands and knees, and we'll find out."

Smiling seductively, I climbed onto the bed and waited for him to take off the rest of his clothes. "I'm ready for you, Arthur."

He dragged the belt through the wetness at my center, making me moan. "I'd say you're more than ready for me."

"I want you. I can't help it."

He pressed himself against my sensitive flesh. "Is that true? Do you want this hard cock, baby?"

I ground myself against his erection, panting and making small mewling sounds in my throat. "Yes, Arthur. Please. Fill me up with that hard cock. I want you to make me scream."

Without another second's hesitation, he plunged into me, filling me with his more than adequate size. "Is this what you want?"

"Yes," I cried out. "Fuck me, Arthur."

He grunted as he obeyed, lifting my knees off the mattress with the force of his thrusts. "That pussy is so wet, so hot. Did you finger yourself for me today?"

"Yes," I moaned as he moved his hands to my breasts.

"Did you think about this fat cock filling your pussy?"

"Yes!" I said breathlessly, feeling his cock growing harder with each stroke. I knew he would come soon. He never lasted long.

Groaning, he said, "Get on your knees, Jasmine."

I slid off the bed and positioned myself in front of him the way he liked, ready to take his cum wherever he decided to put it.

"Finger that wet pussy," he instructed, stroking his cock mere inches from my face. "I want you to come when I do."

"Yes, sir." Reaching down, I started to touch myself. "I'm so close."

"So am I, baby. Come for me."

Dipping inside myself with two fingers, I spread my wetness to my clit and cried out in pleasure.

"That's it," Arthur said, watching my face closely. "Rub that clit, baby."

With one hard working furiously at the hardened nub between my legs and the other pinching my left nipple, it didn't take long for me to scream out a very believable orgasm. Arthur followed close behind, coming on my breasts until he sagged into the chair behind him, exhausted.

"Holy shit." He chuckled to himself.

I smiled. "Are you okay?"

"I'm great. You?"

"You know perfectly well how I am," I teased, getting up to my feet.

He pulled me to him by the hand and kissed my palm. "You were lovely. Next Saturday at the same time?"

"It's a date," I told him.

"Good." He closed his eyes for a second. "I'm thinking crotchless panties and nothing else."

"Sounds like fun. Any more requests?"

"Come twice before I get here. I want you dripping wet."

I grinned. "Yes, sir."

"Now, go take a shower and clean yourself up. I'll wire the money to your account when I get to the car."

"Are you sure you don't want to come with me?"

He gave me a fond smile. "You know I can't stay."

Sighing, I pouted as I walked toward the door. "I know. I guess I'll just have to make do by myself."

He chuckled again. "Saturday, Jasmine. Remember, dripping wet."

"Mr. Evans, have I ever disappointed you?"

His eyes twinkled with humor. "Why do you think I keep coming back?"

CHAPTER FIVE

I showered and blew my hair dry after Arthur left, all the while wondering what Kasper thought about me and my lucrative little business. When I'd checked the outside camera from my room to see if Arthur's car had left, I saw Kasper leaning against the wall outside of the door, hands on his knees, breathing heavily. I didn't understand it. Was what we did that much more difficult for him to watch than the videos I'd assigned him as 'homework'? Arthur was one of my tamer clients. What would he say when he had to witness me with one of the kinkier, dirtier men I serviced?

Kasper didn't leave me wondering for long. He knocked on my office door as soon as he heard the blow dryer go off. I opened the door and smiled at him. "What's up?"

"I think we need to talk," he said, his voice hoarse and gruff.

I frowned. It didn't sound as if I would like what Kasper had to say. "Sure, come on in."

He nodded and walked into the huge bathroom with me, looking around. "So, is this your bat cave?"

"Sort of? Only, I don't fight crime when I leave here. I go home and cuddle with my teddy bears. Again, I'm sorry you had to see that."

He laughed. "No worries. It was rather endearing."

Sitting on the chaise in the adjacent dressing room, I motioned to the chair across from it for him to sit. "What did you want to talk about?"

"I just have some questions," he said.

"Such as?"

He grimaced. "Such as ... how ordinary was what just happened? Is every client so demanding?"

I raised my eyebrows. "You call that demanding?"

"He told you what to do," he said, a little exasperated. "And I thought he was going to hit you with that belt!"

"He wouldn't have done it hard. And even if he did, he paid me well."

"Did he? That's another thing I was wondering. How could you do that without any payment upfront?"

"Yes, he paid. Twenty-five thousand dollars, to be exact. It's not normal for me to do that. He's the only one I'll let get away with it. And that's only because he's my most faithful client. He comes here at least once every two weeks, sometimes more if he's in town."

Kasper sighed. "I honestly didn't know what to do. When he told you to get on your knees and finger yourself, that was one thing, but the belt thing, even with the whip selection on the wall, I didn't know whether I should have stopped him."

I smiled at him. He was so genuinely worried about such a tiny thing. "Look, Kasper. You're going to see a lot you're not going to like. I have one guy who's a peeping Tom, one that likes to touch me while he's playing masseuse, one who wants to pretend I'm passed out during the whole thing, and one guy that ties me up with rope and fucks me while I'm suspended. They're all harmless, and under the circumstances, I'm glad they're coming here to get their jollies instead of bringing that sort of thing into the public."

His eyes bugged out. "Are you serious?"

"One hundred percent serious. One of my regular clients just sent me an email requesting that I fuck someone else before him. I believe the words he used were 'dripping with another man's cum'."

Kasper stared at me, mouth ajar. "Are you going to do it?"

"Probably not. The problem with that is this client wants to see the man that does it. Not in the act, but right after, so he knows the act really took place. My client list is a secret, so I don't think I'll be able to accommodate that particular request."

He sighed. "I don't know how you do this."

"It's easier than you think, especially since ninety-nine percent of the people I'm doing it with are regulars."

"Do they ever ask for anything worse than that?"

"You mean anal?"

He cringed. "No. Well, yes."

"I don't do anal. Not even if the clients request me to do it to them. Assplay is my hard limit."

"There's something I thought I'd never hear."

I laughed. "Kasper, are you going to be okay here? Is this too much for you?"

He shook his head. "I guess I just thought it would be vanilla with an old man."

"I kind of thought that was vanilla."

"You have a strange definition of vanilla."

I lifted my brows. "Okay, then. What would you call vanilla?"

"I thought he would come in, maybe sensually take off your corset, kiss you senseless, then make love to you in the missionary position."

"Is that the way you have sex?" I asked.

He blushed. "Uh, no."

"Then why would you think Mr. Evans would?"

He stood and started to pace. "Because that's what you deserve. You're …" He sighed. "You're just special. You deserve more than that." He motioned around him. "You deserve more than this."

I stood and stopped him from pacing, looking up to his distressed face. "Kasper, you have to understand, I chose this for myself. I'm in control in every single way. And really, none of this is any worse than what you'd see in a porn video. Plus, I get paid well. I can pay my mortgage for a year just from the five minutes I spent with Arthur today. And the guy who emailed me, he's offering seventy-five thousand dollars. I know money isn't everything, but after I get too old for this, I will be able to do whatever I want."

He cupped my face in his hands. "Jasmine, I do understand. I do, but I still don't have to like it."

I rested my palms on his chest. "What would you rather I do?"

"Anything," he said. "Anything would be better than this."

"Kasper, are you going to quit?"

He seemed to come back to himself, realizing that he was holding my face and staring desperately at me. Dropping his hands, he backed away a few steps. "No. Never. Not until you stop doing this."

"You're really worried about me, aren't you?"

"I just want to protect you. I know what's out there. Hell, I've seen what a man tried to do to you. I can't let that happen again. I won't."

"And I appreciate that, but this is what I do. You must come to terms with the fact that I have sex for money. I know hearing that and seeing that are two entirely different things, but it is my chosen profession, Kasper. You can't let your worries get in the way of that."

"I know. I just didn't expect it to be so hard to see it in person. I'm sorry for unloading on you."

I giggled. "Everyone else does. Why not you?"

He shook his head. "You think you're funny, but you're not."

"Please, that was hilarious."

He smirked. "A little. That's all I'm giving you."

I giggled again.

He walked to the door. "All right, I'm shutting up."

"Sorry, Kasper."

He waved a hand but didn't turn around. "Don't be. I'm the one who keeps sticking his foot in his mouth."

"You're only doing it because you care."

"That's the problem with me," he replied. "Always has been."

"Thank you, Kasper. Really."

Sighing, he twisted the knob. "You're welcome. I'll see you on Saturday for Mr. Laughlin."

"See you then."

CHAPTER SIX

When Kasper showed up for work on Saturday, he seemed to be an entirely different person. Gone was the fretting man who was worried about my safety and lifestyle. In his place was a man utterly devoid of concern. He swept into the building with a smile and a chipper attitude that made me a little nervous.

"What's going on with you?" I asked.

Closing the door behind him, he grinned at me. "What do you mean?"

"Two days ago, you were all Debbie Downer. Now you're spreading sunshine wherever you go."

He laughed. "I'm not spreading sunshine."

"If you say so," I said, grabbing my lighter and ashtray from the table next to the door.

"Where are you going?"

I held up my joint. "Outside to smoke."

He eyed my clothing. "Like that?"

I glanced down at my silky robe. "Yeah. I'll be right back."

"Hang on a second. I'm coming with you."

"Okay."

He set down his lunch and shrugged his coat back on. "Are you sure you're warm enough? It's a little chilly out there."

"I'll be fine."

But I was not okay. As soon as I stepped out the door, the wind blowing through the alley between the buildings nearly blew my robe apart. "Shit!"

Kasper laughed. "I told you."

Handing off the joint, lighter, and ashtray, I tightened my robe and tied the sash in a knot. "Holy crap, it's cold!"

He wrapped his arms around me from behind, half covering me with his coat. "Here. Take your stuff. I'll try to keep you warm."

I set the ashtray in the mailbox attached to the cinder block wall and snuggled as close as I could to him. "Won't the smoke bother you?"

"No, I have a prescription for medical marijuana myself."

"Really?"

I felt him shrug behind me. "Yeah. Sometimes, I have nightmares. It relaxes me and helps me sleep through the night."

"PTSD?"

"Yeah."

I didn't know how to respond to that, so I lit the joint and took a long drag.

"Why do you smoke it?" he asked.

"Social anxiety. It loosens me up. I don't know if I could do what I do without it."

"Who's on your plate for today? I didn't see you smoke before Mr. Evans."

"Mr. Laughlin. He's a new-ish client."

"What does he like?"

"He has an oral fixation."

"Like, an oral sex fixation?" he asked.

"Yeah, so far he hasn't wanted to have sex any other way. I think he's self-conscious about his penis. He, unfortunately, has a micropenis. Last time he was here, I talked him into letting me get him off with my hand while I sat on his face."

He shook his head. "I can't believe how casual you are about all this."

"Well, I've been doing it for almost five years," I told him, taking another drag.

"How old were you when you started?"

Blowing out the smoke, I grinned. "Is that a backward way of asking me how old I am?"

He laughed. "Yes."

"I'm twenty-six. I figure I only have another two to three years before I get too old for these guys. I'm thinking of starting a less risqué business after that."

"Really? What kind of business?"

"That, I haven't decided on yet."

"I'm thinking of starting a security company, myself. I have all this extra time during the week. I might as well."

"Maybe I'll invest in your company."

"Maybe we could be partners," he shot back.

I turned in his arms. "Seriously? We barely know each other."

He stared down at me, his blue eyes dark with an emotion I couldn't place. "It doesn't feel that way to me."

"No, I guess not," I said, taken aback. "I do trust you a lot more than I did my last employee, and he worked here for years."

"Why do you think that is?"

"Well, I mean, we've been standing together for a few minutes, and though I can feel how much you want to, you haven't tried a thing. That kind of stuff scores pretty high in my book."

"I can't help the hard-on," he said gruffly. "But I would never force myself on you."

"Not even if I asked nicely?"

His grip tightened around me as he tensed. "It's getting close to showtime. We should go inside and get you warm before Mr. Laughlin gets here."

I smiled, suddenly a little shy. "I'm feeling pretty warm right now."

He chuckled nervously, not quite able to look me in the eye. "Come on, Jasmine. He'll be here in a few minutes."

Kasper headed to his booth after we came back inside, and I went to wait on Mr. McLaughlin in his preferred room. I desperately needed to get my head on straight before he showed up. All I could think about was Kasper. I couldn't help it.

Staring at myself in the mirror, I put on a coat of smudge-proof lipstick and said, "Get it together," seconds before the buzzer rang out, signaling my client's arrival.

I met him at the door, wearing a sheer, pink babydoll nightie that left little to the imagination and nothing else. "Hi, Chris. How's your day going?"

He smiled and sat on the bed to take off his shoes. "It's much better now, Jasmine. You look beautiful, by the way."

I grinned. "Thank you! You look nice, too. You got a haircut since I last saw you."

Absentmindedly, he ran a hand through his sandy brown hair. "Yeah, it was getting a little shaggy. My employees probably thought I was growing a mullet."

I laughed. "It wasn't that bad. I liked the way it curled at the ends."

After patting the bed next to him, he started unbuttoning his shirt. "If I would've known, I would've kept it long for you."

"You're such a charmer," I said, trailing my fingers down his handsome face.

He caught my hand. "You make it easy, Jasmine. Too easy. I thought I was going to have to make another appointment to see you sooner; I was so excited to come here this week."

"You're welcome here anytime, Chris. You know that. And you can always reschedule if you need to."

"Oh, no. I like to space my appointments out. It makes what we do that much sweeter."

"You are just full of compliments today," I remarked, helping him out of his shirt.

"Well, as I said, I've been anxiously awaiting this. I like spending time with you."

Straddling his lap, I ground myself against him. "Likewise."

He groaned and wrapped his arms around me. "I want to taste you."

"Whatever you want," I said, my voice husky.

"I want you just like last time," he told me.

"Will you let me make you come this time?"

He nodded. "I have thought about nothing else since I left last month. That was … amazing."

"Then you should take off your pants. I hated that you had to leave here so messy."

He averted his eyes. "No, I—"

"Chris, there's nothing wrong with you. There is no reason to be ashamed. Let me see you come. I want to."

"Are you sure?"

I smiled. "Of course, I'm sure. I'm hoping one day you'll feel comfortable enough to make love to me, but I understand you need to take it slow. We can work our way up to it."

"I've never had a woman be so nice to me."

I frowned. "I don't know why not. You're good to me. I'm only reciprocating."

He sighed. "Several have laughed at me. One woman I dated told me she wouldn't even feel me inside of her and left the hotel when she saw it."

I pursed my lips. "Have you ever considered that the fault might lie with the women, Chris? I mean, if they won't even give you a chance, why blame yourself?"

"I didn't think of it that way."

"Well, think of it," I said, reaching down to stroke him through his pants. "I know I would feel you. And what's more, I know you would make me come."

"Do you really think so?"

"Yes, and I'm ready to prove that if you are."

"I'd probably come before I even got it in."

"So, what?" I asked, giving him a soft peck on the lips. "The last time you came, you were hard again only seconds later."

"It's hard not to be when I'm around you. You're so sexy." He pulled the string holding my breasts in my nightie and thumbed my exposed nipples. "You're perfect."

I tossed my head back, moaning as I moved against his erection. "I want to feel you inside of me."

Lifting me, he turned us so that I was on my back and he was standing between my legs. "Are you sure?" he asked again.

"Positive," I said, breathless with anticipation.

He unbuttoned his pants and pushed his boxers down, letting them both fall to the carpet. Underneath, he was hard and ready for me.

Sitting up, I slid my hand around the back of his neck to pull him closer. He came willingly, kissing each of my nipples before settling between my thighs. I wrapped my legs around his waist, angling my hips upwards so he'd have better penetration. "Ready?"

He swallowed hard. "Yeah."

I nodded and reached between us to guide him to my entrance, keeping eye contact with him to gauge his reaction. Once he was in position, he moved into me with aching slowness, his first thrust tentative, careful. His second was much more forceful, showing me exactly how much he wanted this.

"Oh my God," he gasped. "You're so hot."

I chuckled sultrily. "I told you. I want you, Chris."

His jaw clenched. "I don't know how long I can—" He broke off, groaning as he pulled out and used his hand to aim for my stomach. "I'm sorry," he panted, resting his forehead on my collarbone. "I just couldn't hold it back."

I ran my fingers through his short hair. "There's no need to apologize. We're not done here. That was just the warm-up."

Lifting his weight, he moved to lie next to me on the bed while I took off my nightie and used it to wipe my stomach dry.

"Sorry," he said again.

I deposited the nightie to the floor and climbed on top of him, letting my wetness slide against his hardening length. "My turn?"

He grinned. "I'll try my best."

"I promise you won't have to try hard," I told him, lowering myself onto his erection and then moving my legs into a reversed missionary position to maximize the sensation for both of us.

"Whoa," he said, breathing heavily.

"Do you like that?"

He grabbed my ass to press me harder against him. "I think 'like' is a vast understatement."

Smiling down at him, I rotated my hips to grind myself against his pelvic bone and gasped when I found the sweet spot I wanted to find. "You feel so good," I told him.

"Come for me," he said, palming my breasts and pinching the nipples lightly. "I want to feel you come on my dick."

That was all it took. I rocked against Chris's cock one more time, then howled out my release, shuddering violently with a long overdue orgasm. Riding out the spasms, I screamed myself hoarse and collapsed onto his chest, breathing hard and fast. "Chris, that was ..."

"Not over," he said, rolling us over and continuing to pump into me.

I squeezed my legs tightly together, chasing that delicious friction, and immediately came again, crying out and digging my nails into his back until he followed me with a loud groan, spilling onto my stomach and breasts.

Sitting back on his knees between my legs, he studied me. "You are magnificent," he told me, panting for breath.

"Get your own lines," I said, laughing. "I was going to say that."

He stood, grabbed a few tissues from the box on the nightstand, and took my hand to help me to my feet. "After that, I might believe you."

"You should," I told him, taking the tissues. "I'm still throbbing."

He smiled. "You're the first I've ever made come that way, you know."

"I find that very hard to believe."

"No, it's true. I've had a few fake it, but even with a small dick, I can feel the difference."

"Well, I am happy to let you feel that difference anytime you want. Wobbly legs are not something you'll hear me complain about."

He chuckled. "How about next week, then?"

I raised an eyebrow. "I thought you liked to spread out our visits?"

"After that, I think I might become a regular. And I might even Google a few new moves. I never thought of doing it the way we did today."

"Hang on," I told him, walking to the bookshelf in the back of the room to grab a book for him.

He perused the cover. "The Kama Sutra?"

"Yes. Find something you think you'll like, and we'll try it out the next time you're in."

"You're on. And, Jasmine?"

"Yeah?"

"Thank you."

I kissed his cheek. "Anytime, Chris. I mean it. Anytime you want."

CHAPTER SEVEN

Kasper knocked on my office door an hour after Chris left. "Jasmine?"

"Hey," I called. "Come on in."

Sitting on the chair I offered, he smiled at me.

I raised my brows. "Why are you smiling at me like that?"

He shrugged. "I don't know."

I sighed. "Please tell me you didn't come in here to make fun of Chris."

He shook his head vehemently. "No, of course not!"

"Then what is it?"

"I guess I just didn't expect what I saw today."

"What part?"

"The part where you brought that guy out of his shell and helped him through his anxiety. You were almost like a sex therapist, a hands-on therapist."

"I told you before that a lot of my clients have quirks. They can't share that with just anyone."

He nodded. "Yeah, but the ones you told me about were fetishes. Mr. Laughlin has a genuine problem, and you helped him."

I smiled. "I didn't mind. It's rare I get to enjoy what I do."

"But didn't you come with the last guy?"

I pressed my lips together. "Well ..."

He gasped. "You faked it!"

I covered my eyes then peeked through my fingers. Kasper was still staring at me, mouth agape. "I can't come on command, Kasper.

I'm not a robot. And Mr. Evans isn't exactly what I would call a caring, devoted lover. He's there to get himself off. That goes faster when he thinks he's doing a good job."

"It's like I don't even know you," he muttered, shaking his head and laughing.

I shrugged. "What can I say?"

"Say that you'll come with me to a barbeque tomorrow. My parents always cook out on Sundays." He wriggled his eyebrows. "You could be my arm candy."

"Are you sure you want me there? That won't be awkward for you?"

"Maybe, if my parents knew what you do for a living, but they don't. All they know is that I work for Locke Enterprises as a security guard."

"Truth evader!" I accused.

Smirking, he picked up an imaginary phone. "Yeah, Mom? Hey. I got a new job today. No, it's not hard. I just watch this hot blonde that I really want to fuck have sex with near strangers. No big deal. Mom? Mom! Stop crying! Mom, you raised me fine. This isn't because you took me out of Sex Ed when I was fourteen. No, Mom. This isn't your fault."

I grabbed his hand and pulled it down to his side. "Hang up the phone, Kasper."

He laughed again. "So, you'll come with me?"

"It depends."

"On what?"

"On whether or not they'll be ribs."

***

When Kasper picked me up at my house the next afternoon, I climbed into his truck fraught with fear that showed plain as day on my face.

"Relax," he told me, giving me a reassuring smile. "They're going to love you."

I wasn't as convinced, but I returned his smile and buckled up. "Okay."

At the first stop sign out of my neighborhood, Kasper stopped the truck and checked behind us before shifting it into park. Turning to me, he asked, "Are you sure you're okay? You haven't said a word since you got into the truck. We could always do this some other time."

I gave him a worried look. "I don't have the best track record with meeting parents."

"There's no pressure, Jasmine. They'll just grill you for an hour or so, ask me when I'm going to make an honest woman out of you, and see if you can fit into my mom's wedding dress."

I gaped at him.

He grinned. "Kidding. I'm just kidding. They'll be normal."

"I hate you," I said sourly.

"No, you don't." He was still laughing as he put the truck in gear and made a right onto Enfield Avenue.

We drove only a block or so down the street before he pulled into the driveway of a bright white, two-story ranch home, cut the truck's engine, and announced, "We're here."

I turned to him, bewildered. "Why didn't you tell me they lived so close? I could've walked here to save you the trouble of picking me up."

"Now why would I do that?" he asked, his voice low and dangerous in its tone.

I met his eyes, feeling a lightning strike of lust shoot through me. I knew that look. Hell, I probably had the same expression on my face right now. It was want, hunger.

"Uh ... s-so, nice h-house," I stammered.

Smiling, he nodded. "I think so. I grew up here."

"Really?" I stared up at the tall trees around the house, wondering what it would've been like to grow up in a place like this. My childhood couldn't have been more different. My mom and I had always struggled, moving from one crappy apartment to the next. "You know, honestly, I thought you'd be from some Scandinavian country with a name like Kasper Johansson."

"No, I'm American, but that is a good guess. Both of my parents are from Stockholm."

"Do you have brothers and sisters?"

"Not one, but my uncle lives next door, and he has two sons that are like my brothers. We're all pretty close in age. What about you? Do you have any siblings?"

"No, it's always been just my mom and me."

"Does she live in Elko?"

"My mom has passed on, but she is buried here in Elko. She was originally from Sparks. She worked as a card dealer at one of the smaller casinos in Reno."

He pursed his lips. "So, it's just you now? You don't have any other family?"

"None living, no. I've been on my own since I was twenty."

He looked away as he pulled the key out of the ignition, then asked, "Is that why you chose to be a sex worker … because you didn't have any other choice?"

I shook my head. "No, I worked two jobs and had my own apartment at eighteen. I chose to be a prostitute to pay for college. At first, I said I'd quit when I graduated, but by the time that happened, I had met a few well-off men who kept recommending me to other well-off men. It seemed silly to quit when the money was so good. Plus, I was having trouble finding a job in my field."

"What is your field?"

"I studied to be a Data Communications Analyst."

He chuckled. "Not much call for that around here in mining country."

I laughed. "Not at all. I could've moved to the Silicon Valley or Austin, but the housing is so expensive, I didn't think it would be worth it in the long run."

"Probably not."

I started to continue our conversation, but a tall blonde woman came out of the front door with her hands on her hips. "Kasper Johansson, you get in here and help your father! He thinks he's Bobby Flay out there on the grill. I'm afraid he's going to burn down the neighborhood!"

Kasper laughed and opened his door. "That's my mom. She's sort of insane."

I smiled. "She seems fine to me."

He sighed. "You say that now. You just wait."

I raised my brows at that and watched Kasper round the truck to open my door. Was he serious?

CHAPTER EIGHT

Kasper whispered quiet, preemptive apologies to me until we came within earshot of his mother, then he took a deep breath before saying, "Mamma, this is my boss, Jasmine Locke. Please, go easy on her."

She waved him off. "Get out there and help your father. Leave Jasmine to me. I'll get her settled in."

He frowned. "I'm serious, Mamma."

"Kasper Håkan Johansson! Are you talking back to your mother?"

"No, ma'am."

"Then do what I said!"

I stared at her, impressed.

She winked. "I've still got it, huh?"

"Yes, ma'am, you do," I replied, laughing at the way Kasper ran into the house like she was going to swat him.

"Oh, let's have none of that," she said with a slight accent. "Call me Annika."

"I'll do that, Annika."

She smiled warmly at me. "Good. Now, let's see how the guys are doing back there."

"Sounds good," I told her, following her into a modern, immaculate living room. "Your house is beautiful."

"Thank you, but I have to be honest. After Kasper told me he was bringing you, I cleaned for two days. A merry homemaker, I am not."

I laughed. "Then, you and I have something in common."

"More than that, I suspect."

My smile faltered a bit. "What do you mean?"

"We both love my son."

"But I don't—"

Annika cut me off with the wave of her hand. "Maybe not yet, but I can see the spark in those pretty green eyes when you look at him."

"But I—"

"If you don't, you will, honey. Just be careful. He's broken a lot of hearts. Let him make the first move."

I nodded, defeated. "I'll be careful, but I don't think Kasper is going to go for me. He knows too many of my secrets."

"Secrets can be kept, doll. And with a beauty like you, I don't think he'll mind."

I chewed my lip. "I don't know, Annika. Mine are pretty big."

She tossed her hands up. "Oh, so what if you're a prostitute? Don't tell my son, but I stripped my way through college. Shit, I think what you have going is a smart, safe way to build up cash while you're still young. I wish I would have thought to do it when I was your age."

My mouth dropped open with a squeak.

She laughed. "Kasper thinks he's slick, but you're dealing with a mom here. Thirty or not, when I see him getting clandestine texts, I'm going to check up on what's going on the first chance I get. All it took was one trip to his house to 'clean' to find the paperwork you'd sent home with him. It didn't take a genius to figure out what kind of job he'd taken."

I shook my head. "You're diabolical!"

"I know it. I should get that printed on a T-shirt."

I grinned. "I know what someone's getting for Christmas."

"I knew I liked you, doll." She wrapped an arm around my shoulders. "Come on. I'll introduce you to my husband, Lucas. Ignore everything he says. He can't help himself."

"Okay."

With something resembling hope, I followed Annika through the kitchen and out the back door to see a tall, graying man and Kasper fussing over a grill. After meeting the amazing woman that was Kasper's mom, I was optimistic that his dad would be equally as understanding if he happened to know about my profession.

Kasper's father sat down in a lawn chair. "So, this is the famed Jasmine Locke! Tell me, lilla du, have you seen my son's kuk yet?"

"His cook? Kasper, you have a cook?"

Annika smacked him on the back of his head. "Lucas!"

"Dad thinks it's funny to say dirty words in Swedish," Kasper told me, giving his dad the evil eye.

"Oh, his cock." Shaking my head, I smiled conspiratorially at him. "Mr. Johansson, if you keep this up, we're going to have to be best friends."

He laughed and elbowed his son. "I like this one. She's not shy like the other ones."

I raised a brow at Kasper. "Just how many girls have you brought to these Sunday barbeques with mom and dad?"

"Two. And full disclosure, not one of those women ever wanted to come back." He jerked his thumb toward his dad. "I don't have to tell you why, do I?"

Lucas laughed. "They were too uptight for you, son. You need a woman who is modig."

"Modig?" I asked.

"It means brave or courageous," Kasper explained.

Lucas pointed a pair of tongs at his son. "Exactly. This girl has pluck."

Annika rolled her eyes. "My love, you're embarrassing our son in front of his guest."

"Our son is a grown man, a military man, Annie. He can speak for himself."

Kasper stood. "That, I can. And I think it's time to go. Jasmine, if you would care to accompany me?"

"Oh, sit down, Kasper," Annika admonished. "You've just gotten here, and the food is almost ready."

He sighed but did as she asked. "Yes, Mamma."

I smirked at Kasper.

"Shut it, you," he growled.

Lucas stood up and retrieved a huge platter of meat. Setting it on the table, he said, "Jasmine, I take it you like meat."

Annika snorted. "Lucas, I said no more of that."

"My blooma, there is no good way to bring up Jasmine's risqué profession. At least, this way, it is amusing."

Kasper, not expecting this conversation, spit out his beer and sputtered, "Wh-what do you m-mean, Pappa?"

He held up his hand, stopping Kasper's indignation. "Son, you don't get to talk until you've apologized to your mother for lying to her about your job."

Kasper looked down and muttered, "Sorry, Mamma."

"That's quite all right, my son. I know why you did it, but you needn't have. I don't mind if Jasmine is a lady of the night."

I grabbed a beer from the cooler and slugged back half of it before I said, "That makes my job sound a lot more glamorous than it is. And besides, I do most of my work during the day."

Lucas cackled. "Oh, but I do like her! Tell us, Jasmine. Have you many clients? What are they like?"

"Not a lot. Maybe seven or eight at the moment. Most of my clientele are regulars, and most of them are around your age."

"Don't get any ideas," Annika said, cutting her husband off from saying what I was sure was going to be something to make things even more awkward.

"You let me have no fun, woman," he complained.

Kasper, finally getting his bearings, asked, "How did you find out?"

"A mother never tells her secrets," Annika replied, then she winked at me.

He looked from his mother to me. "Jasmine?"

I shrugged, my expression one of exaggerated innocence. "A lady of the night never tells her secrets."

He rolled his eyes. "I'm starting to realize I should have never introduced you to my parents."

"Then maybe you'll have better luck with your uncle," a handsome, dark-haired man said as he came out of the back door.

"I don't know if you'll be any better of an influence, Uncle David," Kasper told him dubiously.

The man chuckled. "You might be right about that."

"I know I'm right about that, but I'll introduce you anyway. David, this is my boss, Jasmine Locke. Jasmine, this is my incredibly untrustworthy uncle, David Lanka."

Taking the hand David offered, I shook it. "Nice to meet you. Are you Annika's brother or Lucas's?"

"Neither. I'm just a family friend, really. I was a neighbor to the Johanssons in Sweden. When they wrote to me and told me how nice it was in America, I decided to immigrate as well."

"And has it lived up to the hype?"

"It has, in many ways. For one, as beautiful as the women are in my homeland, the women here in America are much more so.

You, my dear, are absolutely breathtaking. Your features are so exotic. Your figure, so voluptuous."

I smiled and was sure everyone could see my blush. "Thank you, Mr. Lanka."

"Your blush is delightfully innocent, Miss Locke. It is rare to find on a woman these days."

"Oh, I think you'll find our Miss Locke isn't quite so innocent, though I will agree the blush is lovely on her," Lucas told him.

David's eyebrows rose. "Not so innocent, eh? And why is that?"

Kasper started to speak, but I held a hand up to stop him. I didn't need him to lie for me. I wasn't ashamed of what I did for a living. "I'm a prostitute, Mr. Lanka."

"I'm sorry?"

"A prostitute. I sleep with men for money."

"And she's doing a good job of it, too," Annika told him. "I wish I would have been as financially savvy when I was her age."

I grinned at her. "Thanks, Mrs. J."

Kasper looked from me to his mother and then back to me. "What is happening here?"

"What do you mean, son?" Lucas asked. "Can't your mother and I be supportive of the woman you've brought to meet us? Don't you want us to like her?"

"Not if you're going to act like you've been possessed by a couple of sex-crazed co-eds."

I burst out laughing. "Kasper, you do realize your parents had to have sex in order to bring you into the world, right? They're allowed to have a sex life."

"No, I don't realize that, Jasmine, and if you could stop making me think about my parents' sex life, that would be super."

"He's always been such a prude," Annika interjected, rolling her eyes at her son. "I think that time he walked in on us during tantric sex may have scarred him a little."

Kasper stood. "Okay, that's it. I can see that this is going to be another of those 'let's scar Kasper for life' days. If you'll excuse me, I'm going to watch some football."

"Sit down and quit being such a baby," David chided. "Show some dignity in front of the beautiful lady you've brought here today."

"Fine," he muttered, letting out a very put-upon sigh as he sat down. "But if I hear another word about sex involving anyone in this backyard, I'm out."

CHAPTER NINE

"I brought doughnuts!" Kasper called, holding up two bags from Donuts 'N Mor as he walked into the lobby on Thursday morning.

I clasped my hands to my heart in excitement. "Bless you, Kasper Johansson. I'm starving to death in here!"

"I thought you might be. I don't think you eat enough, Jasmine."

"I eat plenty," I said, bouncing up and down in front of him. "What'd you bring me? What'd you bring me?"

"Fruit-filled," he said, holding up his left hand.

I wrinkled my nose. "Gross."

He held up his right hand. "And éclairs."

"Éclairs, please!"

Laughing, he handed me the bag. "You remind me of my parents' old poodle. She used to dance for treats."

"That's the worst compliment … ever," I told him through a big mouthful of sugary goodness.

"Well, she was an adorable poodle."

I feigned thought. "Nope. That's still the worst compliment ever."

"Then, I apologize. Do you think coffee will get me back in your good graces?"

I grinned. "Yes!"

"Good," he said, wiping a bit of chocolate from the corner of my mouth with his thumb. "I'll be right back. I left the cups out in the truck."

"Okay." I happily took another bite and smiled after him as he jogged out the lobby door.

Although we hadn't spoken since Sunday, I felt like the barbecue at his parents had gone very well. And it had certainly been a successful meeting with his parents. We enjoyed each other's company so much, we all stayed up talking until late, even after Kasper had made good on his promise to watch sports if we brought up the subject of sex again.

At first, I felt bad about running him into the house with our sex talk, but I soon forgot all about his discomfort. Discussing my everyday affairs with the Johannsson family had felt natural. There was no condemnation or judgment in their responses, only encouragements. So much so, they made it easy to see where Kasper picked up the relaxed 'live and let live' demeanor he used when his parents weren't embarrassing him to death.

By the time Kasper returned with the coffees, I was digging into the bag for another éclair, while painting the trim around the doorway with my free hand. He watched me for a moment before commenting, "I see you're a multitasker."

I sighed as I glanced at the coffee he was carrying. "If only I had three hands."

"Take a break and eat breakfast with me." When I shook my head and didn't stop, he jiggled the coffee cup in front of my face. "Just a few minutes, Jasmine. I've been meaning to talk to you about something for a couple of days."

"You know we have a lot to do before Mr. Rogers gets here at six, right?"

He snorted. "We'll get it done before Mr. Rogers is in the neighborhood."

"Fine," I said, grudgingly sitting on the edge of the entryway table and taking the coffee he held out to me. "Is this going to be about the visit to your parents' house?"

"Yes."

I cringed, hoping that I hadn't been overconfident. "Okay, let's have it."

He ran a hand through his hair, an uneasy expression on his face. "Did you happen to tell my mom about your decidedly unwholesome vocation before you came outside on Sunday?"

I stared at him, incredulous. "You mean, did I go to your parents' house and tell your mom that you work for a prostitute ten seconds after I met her?"

"Yeah. Did you?"

I shook my head. "No, they already knew about it before I got there."

He tossed his hands up in the air. "But how? Who could have possibly told them? I haven't said a word to anyone."

"Kasper, I think you should give your mom more credit. She's one crafty woman."

He squinted at me. "How do you know how crafty she is?"

"I don't," I said quickly. "Not really."

Without a word of warning, Kasper snatched the éclair from my hand and held it over my head, just out of reach. "You're a terrible liar, Jasmine. What do you know?"

"H-hey!" I sputtered. "Give that back!"

"If you want it, tell me what you know."

"I'll tell you that I will climb you like a tree if you don't give that back," I growled, making an unsuccessful grab for it.

"And I'm saying I'm not giving it back until you tell me," he insisted.

I set my coffee on the table and pounced on him, using his shoulders to try to boost myself up to make another grab at the éclair. "Kasper, this is crazy. Give it back."

Wrapping an arm around my thighs to stop my upward movement, he sighed. "Not going to happen, Jasmine."

I growled. "Kasper, so help me, if you don't give me the damn éclair, I will smother you to death with my breasts."

He laughed and let go of his grip, causing me to slip down.

Unwilling to give up, I wrapped my legs around his waist to stop the downward motion and glared at him. "This is starting to become ridiculous."

"Yes, and it's about to become uncomfortably awkward if you continue to rub your lady parts against my man parts, so why don't you just tell me what you know?"

I chuckled when I felt him growing hard against me. "I think it just got awkward."

Teeth clenched, he said, "This wouldn't be happening if you'd just tell me, Jasmine."

"No," I corrected. "This wouldn't be happening if you'd give me the damn éclair." I smirked. "And if you didn't like my 'lady parts' rubbing against your 'man parts'."

"You think I'm enjoying this?"

I rotated my hips, grinning when he groaned. "I know you are."

He closed his eyes. "Evil woman."

"Evil man," I retorted, shifting myself against him a second time. I desperately wanted to hear him make that sound again.

His eyes popped open. "I'm the evil one? You know what?"

"What?" I asked, my voice nearly a whisper. I was so incredibly turned on.

He lowered his arm as if he was going to relinquish my prize then promptly shoved the rest of my éclair into his mouth.

"You son of a bitch!" I yelled, smacking his chest as I slid to my feet. "I wanted that!"

"And I wanted answers," he countered with his mouth full. "But since you're a brat, let this be a lesson to you."

Huffing, I said, "I hope you get blue balls."

He adjusted himself, smiling winsomely. "I'm getting used to them. Working around here, it's a hazard of the job."

"You think it's a hazard now, you just wait. I'll have you jerking off in the bathroom before you leave tonight."

"Is that a threat, Miss Locke?" he asked, his stare sharp and focused like a predator's.

I poked his chest. "That, Mr. Johansson, is a promise. You will be jacking that big dick as soon as Mr. Rogers leaves. Mark. My. Words."

Stepping closer, he rested his hands on the wall behind me, effectively boxing me in. "You seem sure of yourself."

"You're right," I said, pushing at his chest and meeting his hard stare with one of my own. "I am."

His grin was positively sinful as he asked, "And what makes you so sure you're right?"

I glanced down at his very sizable erection and arched an eyebrow. "Because, baby, you're halfway there already."

"And whose fault is that?" he asked. His eyes were hooded, and his voice was just a growl. He was as turned on as I was.

I shivered as his hot breath moved the fine hairs that had come loose from my ponytail. "Whoever is not keeping you satisfied?"

He swallowed hard. "You think I need to be satisfied?"

I blew out a shaky, shallow breath. "Kasper, if you don't back up a step or two, we're going to both need to be satisfied."

Kasper seemed to come back to himself as he stepped away from me. "I'm sorry."

Sagging with relief, or maybe, disappointment, I leaned my back against the wall and tried to catch my breath. "For what?"

"For … never mind. Let's just get started. We have a lot to do before Mr. Rogers gets here."

My mouth dropped open as I watched him pick up my forgotten paintbrush and get to work. "Are you serious?"

His brow furrowed. "Yeah."

I shook my head as I straightened. "Okay. Just give me a minute. I think *I* may need some alone time in the bathroom."

He didn't reply to my comment as he continued to paint the door trim, but I was sure I saw a small smile on his face as I walked toward my office.

CHAPTER TEN

Mr. Rogers arrived promptly at six o'clock. Like most of my clients, he was a stickler for punctuality. Rich men usually were, and that was fine by me. The sooner they came, the sooner they left. Pun intended.

"You're looking as lovely as ever," he remarked as he walked into the room and looked me over in my skimpy underwear.

"You're looking pretty good yourself," I told him, getting up to kiss his cheek. It wasn't a lie. Tall, tanned, and with a just a tiny amount of salt in his peppered hair, Shawn Rogers was in his prime.

In a deep, rough voice that practically screamed, *"I'm going to rip those panties off with my teeth,"* he said, "I bet you say that to all your men."

"Only when I mean it." I straightened the collar of his dress shirt. "So, Shawn, you traveled all of the way from Twin Falls to see me on a weeknight, which you never do. There must be something you want that couldn't wait until the weekend."

"There is," he said. "Do you remember the roleplaying we did the last time I was here?"

"Of course, I do. I don't think I'll ever forget it." I trailed my fingers down the length of his erect cock. "You nearly fucked me unconscious with this thing."

"And I enjoyed every single minute of it," he growled.

"As did I. Shall we repeat it?"

"No. This time, instead of you being the one who pretends, I want to do it." Pulling a silk mask from his pocket, he held my gaze as he put it on the bedside table. "You know what turns me on. Now I want to know who or what turns you on."

58

I aimed a wicked smile at him. He had no idea the gift he was giving me with this scenario. "That sounds good, but are you sure? You're paying me, not the other way around."

He stepped closer and ran his hands down my bare arms. "Trust me, Jasmine. I'll get my money's worth when I feel that soaking wet pussy on my cock."

I wrapped my arms around his waist. "I have to tell you, Shawn; I am not hating this idea."

"Good." He chuckled as he turned me around to put on the mask. "I've been thinking about this all week. Do you know how many cold showers I've had to take, anticipating this evening with you?"

I didn't reply as I adjusted to the darkness and sight deprivation. I just let him lead me to the bed and listened as he unbuckled his belt and undressed. A minute later, the mattress dipped down with his weight.

"Tell me about him or her," he said, unhooking the front closure of my bra. "What do they look like?"

"He's tall," I told him. "And he has a deep voice."

"What color hair does he have?" he asked.

"Blond."

Cupping my breasts in his palms, he pinched the nipples just hard enough to make me gasp. "Is he handsome? Built?"

"Yes," I whispered, arching into his hands.

"Does he touch you like this?"

I shook my head. "He's never touched me like this. We've never been intimate."

"Never?" he asked skeptically.

"Never."

"Now, how is that possible?" he asked, sliding his hands down my sides to hook his thumbs in my panties. "A woman as beautiful as you, I find that hard to believe."

"We haven't known each other for long," I told him, lifting my hips. "Just a little over a week."

"Still, I have a hard time believing a man would be able to keep his hands ... hell, his mouth off you."

I gasped again and bucked up as I felt his tongue slide against my clit. "Shawn!"

He put a hand on my chest and eased me back down. "I'm not Shawn, remember? I'm the man you desire. Say my name, Jasmine."

"Kasper," I moaned, clutching the duvet as he licked me again.

"Good girl," he said approvingly. "Tell me what you'd like me to do to you."

"Don't stop."

He chuckled again as he lifted my legs over his shoulders and began to lick me in earnest.

Moaning in ecstasy, I threaded my hands through his hair. With the mask tight around my face, it wasn't hard to imagine that it was Kasper's smooth tongue lapping at my core, and after this morning's sexy shenanigans with him, I came with lightning-fast speed, screaming out my completion with unintelligible words in mere seconds.

Before I could catch my breath, Shawn covered my body with his and thrust into my slick wetness, filling me with his broad sex. Pumping hard and fast, he asked, "Is this what you want?"

"Yes!" I cried out loudly.

"Do you like this big cock, Jasmine? I want to hear you beg for it."

"Please, Kasper! Fuck me!"

Rolling me on top, he said, "Take what you want, baby. Make that pussy come again."

He didn't have to ask me twice. I wrapped my ankles around his legs and rode him fast and hard, putting enough friction between us that my clit rasped against his body with every single move. Soon, I was screaming Kasper's name at the top of my lungs.

"Fuck, you're beautiful when you come," Shawn said. "Makes me want to fuck that pouty little mouth of yours."

"Then do it," I told him, sliding off the bed to my knees, where I immediately started to finger myself. "Let me suck your cock, Kasper. I want to taste you."

He scooted to the edge of the bed, and as I wrapped my hands around his dick, he groaned, "Fuck, yes. Suck my cock while you finger that wet pussy."

I didn't hesitate to take him in my mouth. Lost in my lust for Kasper, I yearned for him to come in my mouth, on my face, tits … wherever he wanted. And I longed to make myself come while he did just that.

It didn't take long. No more than a minute later, Mr. Rogers stood, gripping my hair to tip my face skyward. "Open your mouth, Jasmine. I'm going to shoot this big load all over your face."

"Come for me, Kasper," I moaned, working my fingers in and out of me with one hand and using the other to rub my clit. "I want you to come with me."

I felt his come covering my face and tits a second before he roared, "Fuck!"

Crying out with my own release, I wasn't the least bit surprised when he shoved his cock into my mouth to finish himself off. "Suck that fucking cock, baby," he said breathlessly. "Swallow every bit of that cum."

I whimpered as his hold on my hair tightened but took what he gave me gladly. I would have done this and a whole lot more to have the real Kasper's cock in my mouth.

The hold on my hair was finally released when he shuddered with his last spasm and slipped from my mouth. "Jasmine, that was …"

"Awesome?" I said, laughing.

"You have no idea." He tenderly pulled the mask up and used his thumb to wipe away the remnants of his orgasm. "I mean, you're always great, but I've never seen you so into it, so dirty. This Kasper guy is an idiot if he doesn't fuck you, even if you'd likely kill him with all that pent-up lust."

Grabbing his hand, I sucked the cum from his thumb. "Shawn, I'll be as dirty as you want me to be. You know that."

"Yeah, but I like you this way. You're more authentic."

I smiled. "Well, you made it easy."

He collapsed back onto the bed and stared at the ceiling. "Baby, that was not easy. I didn't think I would be able to keep myself together while you rode me. You worked hard for that orgasm."

I crawled over him and nipped at his chest. "Come back next week and make me work for it again."

"I can't next week. But the week after, I'm free. How about that Tuesday, at four o'clock? Pencil me in?"

"I can't wait." Grinning, I ground myself against his cock.

"You're going to have to," he said, though his dick was starting to harden. "I need a second to catch my breath. Can I rest here for a minute?"

"As long as you like, lover. Do you need anything?"

"Yeah. I need you to get yourself cleaned up. I'll see myself out."

I pecked him on the check and got to my feet. "Tuesday after next, Shawn."

"If I can wait that long," he called after me.

CHAPTER ELEVEN

In a completely uncharacteristic move for him, Kasper met me outside of the bathroom door the second I was done showering and brushing my teeth. I wasn't sure if it was because of what he'd witnessed earlier or because I was completely naked, but he looked almost ready to jump out of his skin.

"What's going on, Kasper?" I whispered. "Shouldn't you be watching Mr. Rogers?"

He pointed at the iPad he was carrying. "He just left."

"Oh, then, what's up? Do you need something?"

He backed up to let me out of the door, then started his usual pacing. "Just information."

"Of what sort?" I asked warily.

Stopping in front of me, he crossed his arms. "I need to know if you set that up."

I covered my breasts with my hands and narrowed my eyes. "Set what up?"

"What you did with Mr. Rogers? The roleplaying … was that just to win our little bet?"

"No," I told him honestly. "That was a very happy coincidence."

He shifted uncomfortably. "Happy, huh?"

"Very happy," I purred.

"Fuck, Jasmine," he groaned, staring up at the ceiling.

I glanced down at his jeans, which now had a tiny wet spot of pre-cum. "Did it bother you, what I did?"

"Quite the opposite. I nearly came in my jeans without even touching myself."

"Well, that's … fucking hot."

He grimaced. "You have no idea what it was like to have to sit through that. Every time you said my name, my dick pulsed like it had a mind of its own."

I shrugged. "Sounds like you need to take care of things. You can go home if you're ready."

"Yeah, I know, and I will, but this seemed like a teachable moment, so I decided to come to talk to you first."

I raised my brows. "Teachable moment?"

He handed me the iPad. "Room one. Two minutes. Get comfortable."

"Wait. What?" I asked, watching him hightail out of the door.

"Two minutes," he called over his shoulder.

"Okaaay," I muttered, sitting on the chaise and bringing up the camera in room number one.

Kasper appeared in the room less than a minute later and nodded at the camera. "Can you hear me?"

I tapped the microphone button. "Yes, but—"

"Shhhhhhh," he said, stripping off his shirt.

My eyebrows lifted in surprise. Was Kasper about to do what I thought he was going to do? My mouth dropped open as I watched him kick off his shoes and pop the button on his jeans.

Yep. He was doing what I thought he was doing.

He looked up at the camera and grinned. "I was going to do this in the bathroom, but then that would make you right. Can't have that now, can we?"

"Apparently not," I said sourly.

"Don't be that way, Jasmine. You need to know how hard this is for me."

"I think I already know how hard you are," I told him.

"Do you?" he asked, pushing his jeans and boxers down his thighs. "Because I'm pretty sure you haven't seen my cock before." He sat on the bed with his back to the headboard, displaying everything to me.

My breath caught as I took in how big and beautiful his hard cock was. "Nope, you're right. I would remember seeing that. I'm pretty sure this will be permanently etched in my memory from now on."

He smiled. "Good. Because I'm about to ask you to do something you're not going to want to do."

"What's that?"

"Don't touch yourself while I'm doing this. No matter how much you want to. Keep your hands on the iPad until I tell you that you can come."

"Seriously?" I cried.

"Seriously. I want you to know exactly how I feel when I have to watch you touch yourself or fuck those men."

I sighed. "You were one of the torturers at Guantanamo Bay, weren't you?

He laughed. "No. Now be quiet so I can concentrate."

"Zipping it."

He smirked. "But not touching it, right?"

"No, not touching it. But if I spontaneously combust, you'll know who is to blame."

"You won't die," he told me, palming his erection. "I should know."

I blew out a deep breath and watched him stroke his long length. "Ten seconds after you come, I'm finding my favorite vibrator."

"After I come, you can fuck yourself cross-eyed, Jasmine. But right now, I want your beautiful mouth to shut, both of your hands on the iPad, and both of your eyes on this big, hard dick."

"Yes, sir," I whispered, not about to disobey. I wanted to see him come more than I'd ever desired anything in my life.

Kasper reached into the bedside nightstand where he knew there was a fresh supply of lube, and then squeezed a liberal amount of the clear liquid into his palm. Looking up at the camera, he gave me a sly smile before he slowly spread it along his length.

Transfixed, I watched his stomach muscles contract and release as he pumped his hand from base to tip.

"Is this cock what you were thinking about when you made yourself wet for Mr. Evans?" he asked as he began an easy rhythm. "Was it what you were thinking about when you came with Mr. Laughlin?"

Biting my lip, hard, I choked down my moan as my center began to dampen with want.

"Is it, Jasmine?" he continued. "Do you want this big cock inside of that wet pussy like you told Mr. Rogers? Or maybe, in that sweet mouth of yours?"

Clutching the iPad so tight I heard it crack, I stared at his hand as it slid over the slick skin, wanting to feel it inside of me so much, I could barely stand it.

A subtle sheen of sweat broke out over his taut body as he picked up the pace. "I wonder if you'd let me come inside of you, Jasmine. I'd fill you up. I'd fill you up and then fuck you again. I wouldn't stop until you begged me."

As I watched him stroke faster and faster, I felt wetness on the inside of my thighs. Just listening to him made me so wet, I knew I would never beg him to stop fucking me. I'd fuck him until neither one of us could keep going.

"I'm going to come, Jasmine. Are you ready to touch yourself? Answer me."

"Yes," I groaned. "Please, hurry."

He chuckled. "Just a few more seconds. Are you going to think about this cock while you fuck yourself?"

"Yes. Please come, Kasper. I need to—"

"Do what I'm about to do?" he asked.

"Yes," I breathed out.

"Good," he growled before tensing up with his orgasm. "Fuck!" he roared, pumping himself hard and fast.

A desperate sound escaped me as I watched cum cover his stomach and chest. With every one of his strokes, I felt closer and closer to having my orgasm. I squeezed my thighs together. I wasn't even going to need the vibrator. I would come as soon as he let me touch my clit.

Kasper collapsed back onto the headboard. "Go ahead," he said breathlessly. "But this time, Jasmine, know it's me making you come."

As soon as he commanded it, I dropped the iPad and began to work my clit as if I'd never come again. I came almost immediately, crying out his name over and over until I was hoarse, limp, and sated.

CHAPTER TWELVE

I took my third shower of the day—a quick, cold one—and met a similarly wet-haired Kasper in the lobby. He was wearing an expression I couldn't figure out. It wasn't smugness like I thought I'd see. It was more like a military man's acceptance of something he hadn't expected but was dealing with the best he could.

"Hey," he said, eyeing my sheer shirt and pencil skirt. "Where's your coat?"

"Hi," I said, not quite able to hold eye contact with him. "I forgot it again. I was in a hurry to get out of the house this morning."

He shrugged his coat off and put it on my shoulders. "Here. It's still really chilly out."

"Thanks." After putting my arms through the sleeves, I zipped it up as we walked to the door.

He stopped me with a hand on my shoulder. "Jasmine, are you okay?"

"I'm fine," I assured him, finally meeting his gaze. "Just a little embarrassed."

He frowned. "I'm sorry. I shouldn't have done what I did. I was just so worked up; I wanted you to know what it's like for me."

"No! What you did was understandable. I shouldn't have done what I did! You told me blue balls were a hazard of the job, and I purposely made it harder on you." I sighed. "I suck."

He held up his hands, one of which had a perfectly rolled joint between the index and middle fingers. "Okay, can we just agree that we both mishandled things?"

I snorted. "You said, 'mishandled'."

He snickered. "Well, you said, 'I suck'."

I shook my head at our ridiculousness. "Aren't we supposed to be goofy like this after we smoke?"

"I'm not sure what the protocol is in this situation."

"Ugh. What is wrong with us?" I asked, burying my face in my palms.

Kasper pulled my hands down. "Nothing is wrong with you. Me? I'm not so sure. This job is a lot tougher than I imagined it would be."

I met his gaze. "Are you going to quit? I don't want you to quit."

"No, but I am going to ask for some time off tomorrow."

"Going to the unemployment office?" I asked.

He slung an arm around my shoulders. "No, I really do have an appointment. I'll be in around eleven or twelve to help ready the rooms for the next few days."

"Mr. Evans," I said with another heavy sigh.

"I'm getting the feeling you don't like him."

"He's nice enough, but he has that stupid thing about me getting wet before he gets here. He could just take the time to do it himself."

"So, he's a selfish lover. It could be worse."

"For sure," I told him. "And I really shouldn't complain. Mr. Burl comes tomorrow, so I get a little bit of a reprieve from my more demanding clients."

Opening the door, Kasper led me out. "Mr. Burl? I don't think you've mentioned him."

"I have. He's the guy with the masseuse fetish."

He handed me a perfectly rolled joint and a lighter. "Even so, it sounds like you need this more than me."

"Thanks." Turning my back to the wind, I struck the lighter. "Nice roll, by the way."

"Thanks, but I can't take the credit. I used a rolling machine."

"Cheater."

Kasper laughed and took the joint from me. "I know." He took a drag and held it in for a second. "So," he began, blowing the smoke upward, "are we okay?"

"Perfectly so." I took the joint, hitting it before adding, "I think we might be better than we were before. We've gotten all of the formalities out of the way and shown each other our less than perfect selves."

His brows winged up. "You know, that's a very astute take on the situation."

I handed the joint back and coughed. "Uh … thanks?"

"I just meant …" He sighed. "Hell, I don't know what I meant. I'm just glad you aren't firing me for sexual harassment."

I laughed. "I rubbed my lady parts on you earlier, remember? So I don't think I'm in any position to judge."

After taking another hit of the joint, he stubbed it out on the cinder block wall. "Yeah, well, you didn't hear any complaining about you rubbing your lady parts on me, did you?"

"No, I—"

"Hey," he interrupted, looking down the street. "Where's your car?"

After a second of panic, I remembered the flat tire I'd had the night before. "It's in the shop. I messed up the rim when I had a flat last night. I took an Uber here this morning, which reminds me, I have to order one in a second."

"I can give you a ride home."

"In your condition?" I asked, looking pointedly at the roach in his hand.

"How about I take you to dinner first? The Basque place is right around the corner. We can walk."

"All right. I'll grab my purse and meet in a minute?"

He nodded. "Sounds good."

***

"Well, I could eat all of this," I said, tracing my finger down the right side of the menu. "I'm so hungry."

He shook his head. "No more pot for you."

"That was about all I could smoke, anyway. I'm a total lightweight."

"That is obvious."

I reached across the booth to smack his arm. "Rude!"

He grinned. "I'm just kidding. I like you like this."

"Like what?" I asked.

He shrugged. "Uninhibited, I guess."

"I find it hard to believe that you ever think I'm the opposite, especially with my job."

"Oh, you're definitely uninhibited sexually, but emotionally, you're a little shutdown. I like it when you loosen up and don't worry about what other people are thinking."

Sitting back, I thought about that for a minute. Was I really that closed off? Was that why Mr. Rogers had said he liked me when I was more authentic? Was it because I let myself feel and do things I usually wouldn't? If that was the case, I needed to work on my acting skills. I couldn't have my clients thinking I wasn't enjoying it.

Of course, with clients like Mr. Evans, it didn't matter. They just took what they wanted and left. I guess they were a little shut off themselves.

"You okay?" Kasper asked. "I didn't say anything wrong, did I?"

"No, not at all. I just realized you're right."

He nodded but didn't comment, which made me wonder what else he thought about me that I didn't know.

"Kasper?"

He glanced over. "Jasmine?"

"I'm Mr. Evans, aren't I?"

His forehead furrowed. "Huh?"

"I'm selfish and self-centered. I take what I want and don't care about anyone else."

"That's not true."

"Are you sure? I mean, you know all about me. Hell, you've seen all of me, but what do I know about you?"

"You know what I look like naked, too," he reminded me.

"Yeah, but besides what I learned about you from your parents, what have I asked about you? I haven't even tried to get to know you. I don't know what you did in the Army. I don't know what you do for fun. I know absolutely nothing because I didn't even think to ask. If that's not selfish, I don't know what is."

"I don't know what you do for fun," he pointed out.

"I don't have fun. I fuck men and go home and feel out of sorts while I watch *Gilmore Girls*. What do you do?"

"Same."

I poked him in the ribs. "Liar."

He grinned. "I don't have many hobbies. I work out in the yard, tinker with an old GTO I have in my garage, and watch movies. I'm a homebody."

"We have that in common."

"But I'm sensing you're not happy, Jasmine."

I crossed my arms in front of my chest, feeling a little vulnerable. "I think I'm lonely, Kasper. I don't have any friends or loved ones. I don't even have a pet. I feel ... adrift."

"I know how that can feel. I lived at home until I did basic and my military police training at Fort Leonard Wood in Missouri. There, it didn't seem so isolated. There were a ton of guys, and we had a pretty good camaraderie going. But when I was stationed at Fort Carson in Colorado, I felt alone. A lot of the other guys had wives and kids. I had no one."

I frowned. "That sounds miserable."

"It was miserable. That's why I left after four years. I wanted to settle down, find a wife, have a few kids … just be normal."

"But that didn't happen?"

He chuckled. "No. It turns out, girlfriends aren't something you can order off the internet. There's actual work involved in wooing them. And not many of them want someone who has issues like my PTSD. Plus, I'm a little picky about the women I date."

I sat up straighter, my interest piqued. "Oh?"

"Yeah. The women can't be drunks or drug addicts, and my mom must approve of them. She's a great judge of character."

"I can see that about her," I said, grinning. Kasper's mom was one of the most interesting women I'd ever met.

"She likes you, you know? She asks about you every time I call her."

"Really? I like her, too. She is hilarious. And so is your dad. He's totally inappropriate, but that's part of his charm."

"He'd love to know you think that. The last girl I brought to their house accused him of sexual harassment and wanted me to take her home because he made an off-color joke. It wasn't even one of his risqué ones."

"Well, she sounds like a lot of fun."

He shook his head and laughed. "Not even a little bit. That's the last time I pick up a woman at a protest."

"What was she protesting?"

"Honestly, I can't even remember," he said, turning his smile on the approaching waitress. "I'll have the Basque pork chops and fries.

"Same, please." I handed her my menu. "Thanks."

When the waitress left, he continued, "Bianca was unhappy with a lot of things. In the short time I was with her, she had me drop her off at the slaughterhouse, so she and her friends could make customers feel bad that cows were dying. Then she had me drop her off at the Starbucks, so she could berate the town for buying coffee from them instead of the mom and pop businesses. And the last time, I took her to the local high school to protest the mascot being an Indian."

My eyes widened. "Wow."

"Yeah, I got yelled at for things I'd never even thought about before."

"That doesn't seem like the kind of girl you'd settle down with," I said, taking a sip of water.

"No? Then what kind of girl do you think I'd settle down with?"

"I'm thinking an ex-cheerleader type with close family connections, a small dog in her handbag, and possibly, a high-pitched baby voice."

His brows raised in surprise. "You came up with that pretty quickly."

I shrugged. "I call it like I see it."

"Well, you're calling it wrong," he said, tucking a lock of my hair behind my ear. "Lately, I've found myself very interested in a petite blonde with remarkably green eyes and a tongue that could cut paper."

Lost for words, I stared up at him. Was he serious? I knew Kasper and I had chemistry like crazy, but what he was talking about was more than attraction. He was talking about a relationship, settling down. How could he possibly want something like that with me?

He moved closer to me, concern in his expression. "Jasmine?"

"Yeah?" I squeaked, alarmed at his sudden proximity.

"Is this okay?" he asked, cradling my face in his hands. "Do you want this?"

My heart was beating fast, and my breath was nearly coming in pants, but I answered him truthfully. "Yes."

With a curt nod, he lunged for my mouth, hungrily molding his lips to mine. I sighed and sank into the kiss, letting him sweep his tongue into my mouth as I clutched his shirt in my fists like he was a lifeline. When he pulled back, I was dazed, breathless. And I wanted more.

"Kasper, I …"

"Me, too," he said, kissing me again, this time, chastely.

Kasper slid back to his side of the table and smiled at me, looking like the cat that had eaten the canary.

"What?" I asked.

"Nothing. I just can't wait to see you tomorrow."

I shook my head. "You're seeing me now."

He squeezed my thigh, then laughed when I jumped. "Yes, but tomorrow is an entirely different day."

CHAPTER THIRTEEN

I woke up on Friday morning even more of a worried wreck than I'd been the day before. Kissing Kasper had thrown my whole world out of whack. And as I lay there, staring at the ceiling and trying to make peace with my warring emotions, I realized I was afraid. I was fearful that Kasper would regret the kiss we'd shared, that he would show up after his appointment and give his notice. Hell, I was afraid he'd pack his bags and move to Timbuktu the second he realized he had kissed me only a couple hours after another man had his dick in my mouth.

After a few more minutes of inner turmoil, I sucked it up (no pun intended) and rolled out of bed with courage and strength I didn't think I had in me. Despite my fears, I knew I had to hold my head up high. I couldn't let myself go spiraling off course with my worry that Kasper would change his mind about me. I'd been strong enough to be without a man for years. Some Johnny come lately wasn't going to ruin my confidence … no matter how perfect he was or how much I liked him.

Shaking off the agonizing anxiety, I showered and took extra care with my appearance, straightening my hair, spending an exorbitant amount of time on my eyeliner, and trying on outfit after outfit. But no matter what I tried on, nothing seemed good enough for Kasper. I knew that had little to do with the style of the shirt I wore, that it had everything to do with the fact that I was a whore and he could do a hundred times better than me, but I was still determined to make an impression. Even if he decided he didn't want me, I would floor him today.

Finally deciding on a deep red wrap dress that showed just enough cleavage, I slipped into black pumps and my coat and opened the front door to watch for the Uber driver picking me up at ten o'clock. As I waited, I heard a familiar truck rounding the corner to my street—Kasper's truck. Confused, I stepped onto the porch just as he pulled into the driveway and jumped out.

"What are you doing here?" I asked, trying desperately to appear nonchalant. "I thought you had an appointment."

"I did, but when I got to the doctor's office, they told me I didn't have to be there for the results of my tests. They had already emailed them out."

"That was a wasted trip," I said, curious why he'd seen the doctor. I hoped it wasn't anything serious.

He shrugged. "Not really. It put me going past your house at the right time. Need a ride to work, pretty lady?"

I smiled at the compliment. "I called an Uber, but I can cancel it without a fee. He's over five minutes late."

"Why don't you do that and hop in the truck with me. Have you eaten breakfast?"

"No, but I can't. I don't have time."

He frowned. "Are you sure? You barely touched your food last night."

"Well, in all fairness, a sexy man masturbated in front of me then surprised me with a smoking hot kiss last night. It's hard to think of anything else right now."

Kasper grinned as he opened the passenger side door for me. "Same here."

A thrill ran through me as his words sank in, but I still couldn't stop myself from making a joke at his expense. "A sexy man kissed you and masturbated in front of you, too? What are the odds?"

He barked out a laugh. "You think you're funny, Jasmine."

"No," I corrected, "I know I am."

He shook his head and muttered, "Silly thing," as he closed my door.

In total delight, I grinned at my cheekiness and checked a new notification on my phone as I waited for Kasper to make his way around the truck and get settled.

"So, where would you like to go?" he asked, buckling his seatbelt.

"Really, I can't," I said, opening my email app. "I have Mr. Burl coming in less than an hour. He called to change his time last night."

He frowned. "And you didn't tell me?"

"You had a doctor appointment. And besides, Mitchell has been a client for years. He always does the same thing, like clockwork. He's the last client I would ever worry about."

"Okay. Work, it is. But afterward, you're getting something to eat, and while you're eating, you're going to promise me that you won't have sex without me in the building, okay? I don't care how long he's been a client. You need security there."

"Yes, sir," I teased, then I gasped as I glanced down to read the email from the service I used to handle my client's tests and background information. Stunned, my eyes widened as I read. "K-Kasper?"

His brows furrowed. "Jasmine? Are you okay? What's wrong?"

I stared at him, incredulous. "You ... you applied to be a client?"

"Well, yeah," he replied, looking a little embarrassed. "I knew you'd need proof that I don't have any issues if things ... uh, progressed too quickly. Your business depends on you being diligent about your health."

My heart thumped loudly in my ears. "But the process takes a week. When did you do all this? And how did you do it without me knowing?"

"I found the paperwork in the security office. I filled it out, sent it in, and went for testing the day after Mr. Evans came in."

"Seriously?" I asked, dumbfounded.

"Yeah." He pursed his lips and met my eyes. "Are you upset that I did it without asking you first?"

"No," I said, shaking my head in wonder. "Just surprised, I guess. I knew we had an intense attraction to each other, but I didn't know you were looking for something serious until last night."

"I was only a bit hopeful at the beginning," he admitted, cranking the truck. "But when you said you were having impure thoughts about me at the Mexican restaurant, I knew I was going to go for it. I don't have the money to be an actual client of yours, but I thought there might be some real chemistry between us, so I took a chance."

"I would never ask you for money, Kasper. You know that." I hesitated. "I hope you know that."

"I know you wouldn't," he assured me.

"Good," I said, looking away.

"But?"

I met his eyes. "But what if …" I trailed off, not knowing how to finish the question.

"What if I can't handle you fucking other men for money?" he supplied.

I cringed, hating the way that sounded coming out of his mouth. "Yeah."

He shrugged and put the truck into reverse. "We'll figure it out."

"You say that now, but what if you change your mind?"

He put the truck back into park. "Jasmine, I won't change my mind. I've thought about nothing but this for a week. I even talked to my mom about it last night. I'm committed to seeing if we have something worth pursuing."

"Are you sure?" I pressed. "If you're just doing this to get laid, you don't have to. I'll fuck you if that's what you want."

He held up a hand to stop me. "I don't want to just fuck you. I mean, yeah, I want to fuck you. I want to fuck you in the cab of this truck, right here in your driveway. But more than that, I really like you, Jasmine. I go home at night and wish you were there. I wonder what you're doing, whether you're thinking of me. I tried to wait it out, to let you make the first move, but honestly, I didn't think you ever would. You're too shy, too sweet. You put on this confident front, but I can see what's beneath the sex appeal and flirtation. I know you. I've seen you in a way no one else has."

His words were so heartfelt, they made my chest ache. "Kasper, I never expected any of this. I don't know what to say."

"Say you'll go out with me and only me. I don't mind sharing your body with your clients, but I want all of your heart."

I gave him a small laugh. "That's either the sweetest thing anyone has ever said to me or the creepiest."

"Let's go with sweetest." Leaning in, he brushed a soft kiss on my lips.

I smiled and breathed in his scent before kissing him back, marveling at the warmth of his full lips against my own. When I pulled away, I whispered, "Sweetest, it is."

CHAPTER FOURTEEN

"So, do you massage Mr. Burl, or is it the other way around?" Kasper asked, holding up a pair of red lace panties and wriggling his eyebrows.

Rolling my eyes, I snatched the panties from him and stuck them back into the dresser drawer. "The other way around. I'm not going to lie. He's probably one of my favorite clients. I get a thorough massage and an orgasm every time he visits."

Kasper's eyebrows shot up. "Really? Does he fuck you to orgasm?"

"He's never fucked me. He fingers me until I come, then I deep throat his dick with my head hanging off the table while he massages my tits."

"That's … um, oddly specific. Does he ever ask you to massage him back?"

"Never. Mitchell doesn't speak, and from what I gather, he doesn't like to be touched."

He shook his head and headed for the door. "I don't understand some of these guys. Who wouldn't want to be touched by you?"

I shrugged. "Everyone has their own quirks, I suppose."

"Maybe," he said, making his way to the door. "But I still don't get it. See you in five?"

"Five," I responded, my mind already on what was to come as I sat down at my vanity table and stared at myself in the mirror. It had taken everything I had in me to prepare myself for Mr. Burl. Even though he was a favorite of mine, it wasn't him I desired. I wanted the blond man with the sarcastic smirk and mischievous dark blue eyes whose taste was still on my lips, and I wanted him badly. But first, I had to let a middle-aged man touch me for money.

Sighing, I stood and gave myself one last look. My blonde hair was straight and perfectly styled. My makeup was applied lightly to emphasize my natural beauty. Like always, I'd done everything I could to be perfect for the part. Now I just had to play it.

With a grimace, I dragged myself down to the third room where Kasper was waiting for me. He smiled when he saw me, but it didn't reach his eyes. I could tell that, just like me, he wanted to be the one who touched me today, the one who made me cry out as he brought me to orgasm with his fingers.

"Are you ready?" he asked. "It's time."

I shed my robe and laid it across the foot of the bed. "Yeah."

His eyes raked my body as I moved across the room to him. I felt hot and feverish under his stare. "Like what you see?" I asked, half-joking and half-wanting him to bend me over the massage table and fuck me right here.

Kasper licked his lips and pulled me by the waist into the warmth of his body. His cock was hard and ready as it pressed into my stomach. "I want you to think about me when he touches you, Jasmine. If he makes you come, I want you to imagine it's me."

Sliding my hands around the nape of his neck, I said, "I haven't thought about anyone else but you since we met."

His smile was all male as he leaned his head down to brush his lips across mine. "Good."

I let my hand slowly graze down his abdomen to his erection, enjoying the sharp hiss that burst out of him. "No, Kasper, 'good' would be you throwing me over this table and fucking me hard and fast."

All of Kasper's restraint seemed to leave him in the space of a breath. He kissed me roughly, pushing me against the table with his big body and bending me backward with the intensity of his kiss. Then as fast as it began, it was over. Groaning, he took a step back. "Don't tempt me, Jasmine."

"Later?" I panted, my breasts heaving.

"Soon," he corrected. "Very soon. Now get up on that table. He'll be here any second."

"If I must," I grumbled petulantly, standing up on my tiptoes for one more kiss from him before climbing onto the table to lay on my stomach.

"Fuck, you're beautiful," Kasper said, his voice nearly a growl as he trailed his fingers from my ankle to the curve of ass. "I almost don't want to cover you with this towel. It seems a shame to deprive Mr. Burl of this sight when he walks in."

I let out a shaky sigh. My body was positively vibrating from the intensity of the lust coursing through me. "Go, Kasper, before I put that hard cock to use."

His smile was a promise of satisfying sex and multiple orgasms as he placed the towel over my bare ass. "Jasmine, if I had the time, I would fuck you into a sex coma with this hard cock."

"If only," I lamented.

Kasper had only left the room a moment or two before he alerted me to Mr. Mitchell Burl's arrival. I was calm as I instructed him to give him entry, but, secretly, I couldn't wait for my client. After the kiss Kasper had just laid on me, I felt like I would implode if I didn't have an orgasm soon.

As usual, the tall, dark, and handsome businessman was silent as he entered the room, only taking a moment to let his kind, brown eyes graze the length of my body as he took off his shirt, shoes, and jacket and folded them into a neat pile he placed on a chair next to the door. Then with quick but quiet footsteps, he approached the table wearing only a pair of loose-knit yoga pants, his dick hard and straining against the fabric to be released.

I closed my eyes and allowed myself to fully relax onto the table as I heard him pick up the decanter of warmed oil and couldn't stop the moan as it hit my skin. This was the best part of Mitchell's visits—the sensual feel of him slowly dripping the oil from the nape of my neck, down my back, and then letting it pool hot and wet between my legs. It never got old.

Mitchell's breath was shallow as he moved his strong hands over my shoulder and dug his thumbs into the muscle. I could only groan and squeeze my thighs together as the tension melted away and was replaced by pure desire. I wanted more, and he was never one to disappoint. His talented hands kneaded their way from my shoulders to my back, down my ribcage, and finally, to the edge of the towel, where he paused his movements as if asking permission.

I lifted my head and met his dark, hungry eyes. "Don't stop."

Nodding, he dipped down under the towel, expertly massaging my hips, my ass, and my inner thighs, all the while letting his thumbs come closer and closer to my center with every circular motion. I bit my lip, focusing on the motions, trying to anticipate the moment he would give me what I wanted. And fuck me, I wanted it. It was all too easy to pretend the hands touching me were Kasper's, that the rock-hard dick at my eye level was the one I craved.

"Please," I begged, unable to stay still. "I want to feel you inside of me."

Mitchell's eyes flared, and he immediately plunged his right thumb into me, using the thumb of his other hand to stroke my clit. I gasped and ground myself against his hands, chasing the sensations with my hips. I was already so close, so ready to let myself go. But after only a few blissful seconds, he moved his hands and patted my ass, signaling a position change. I languidly turned over to my back, crying out and arching upward when he poured more oil over my already soaked pussy and gently pushed two long fingers inside of me. Smiling slightly, he caressed my breasts and watched me contort my body under his touch, my moans of pleasure getting louder and louder until I froze and cried out as my release shot through me like lightning.

Sated, I felt boneless as he pulled me backward on the table so that my head hung down in front of the weeping cock he'd pulled out of his loose-fitting pants for me to suck. Taking him in my mouth, I let him angle my head the way he liked, and he slowly canted his hips, barely sliding the head past my lips before he pulled back and pushed his way back in.

After a few of those small thrusts, Mitchell groaned loudly and pushed in deeper until his cock was fully engulfed in my mouth and throat. Pausing to shudder, he palmed my breasts and plucked at my hard nipples as he carefully fucked my mouth over and over. Soon, his breathing grew labored and heavy, and less than a minute later, he seized up all at once and spilled his release down my throat.

When he got his breathing under control and was able to move, he tucked himself back into his pants and walked around to the side of the table to help me sit up. His face was a myriad of emotions as he gingerly used his thumb to wipe the remnants of himself from the corner of my mouth.

"Thanks," I told him, smiling up at him.

Nodding, he returned the smile, quickly made his way over to the neatly stacked pile of his clothes, studiously got dressed, and left the room before I could try to make awkward, one-sided small talk.

Hearing the door close behind him, I slumped in relief and sighed. No matter how many times we did this, the uncomfortable silence after we were together was always hard for me.

A few seconds later. Kasper spoke over the intercom. "He's gone."

"Cool," I said, hopping off the massage table. "I'm going to shower. See you in a minute?"

"Sure. Unless you want me to join you."

My steps toward the door faltered as I wondered if I had heard him correctly. "What did you say?"

His voice was low and sensual as he replied, "I asked if you needed any help in the shower."

I smirked at the camera. "Naughty boy."

"I can't help it. You have no idea how good you look right now."

Glancing at my oily, naked body in the two-way mirror, I shrugged. "I'm not seeing it."

"Well, I am, and it's hotter than hell."

"Speaking of hotter than hell," I said, my empty stomach rumbling. "I would do unspeakable things to you if you'd order a pizza for me. Order two if you want some."

He laughed. "If I would have known all it takes to get 'some' was pizza, I would've ordered it days ago."

I rolled my eyes and started for the door. "Pepperoni, smartass."

"Your wish is my command, boss lady."

CHAPTER FIFTEEN

The pizza had already arrived by the time I joined Kasper in the front lobby. While he waited on me to get out of the shower, he had spread a sheet on the floor and distributed paper plates and napkins. Two ice cold bottles of Coke were in the middle next to the two opened boxes of pepperoni.

Sighing happily, I sat down. "This looks like heaven."

He grinned at me from where he sat against the wall. "I'm glad you approve."

"There isn't much you do that I disapprove of. You're kind of perfect when it comes to this kind of thing."

"Can you say that in front of my mom the next time we're at my parents?"

"Aww. It's cute you think there's help for you where that's concerned."

He sighed as he leaned forward and grabbed a piece of the pizza. "A guy can dream, right?"

I rolled my eyes. "You know your mom adores you. You have her eating out of your hands."

Holding the slice of pizza close to my mouth, he asked, "What about you?"

I took a bite of what he offered and chewed before saying, "Me? I think you just want to put things in my mouth."

"Well, you're not wrong there," Kasper replied, laughing.

"I knew it," I told him, smacking him lightly on his thigh.

"Hey, I've seen what you can do with that mouth."

I smirked as I put a slice of pizza on my plate. "Don't get any big ideas about doing what Mitchell just did. Your giant-sized dick would never fit down my throat."

His brows rose. "I'm not sure if that's a compliment or something I should be disappointed about."

"Take it as a compliment. You have a really nice penis from what I saw on the camera, which makes me wonder why you're still single. Who would want to give up that monster?"

"I'm single because I'm looking for the right woman," he said, chuckling and shaking his head. "I don't want to string women along if I don't plan on committing."

"That's nice of you," I noted. "Not a lot of guys would do that."

"Pussy isn't everything."

"Yeah," I picked up my pizza to take a bite, "there's also food."

He pointed his own pizza slice at me for emphasis and said, "Exactly."

Smiling at him, I turned my attention to my plate, filling it several more times before I admitted defeat. Kasper watched me intently the entire time, his face rapt on mine as he finished two more slices and took a swig of Coke from his bottle.

"You're not eating much," I remarked, consolidating the pizza into one box.

He met my gaze, his blue eyes twinkling with humor. "I'll eat something later."

My mouth quirked up into a half grin. "That sounds like fun."

He laughed at my expression. "Get your mind out of the gutter, Jasmine."

"I can't help it," I protested, pouting prettily. "I desperately want to know what you feel like when you're inside of me."

He groaned and adjusted himself. "Trust me, Jasmine. You'll be finding that out soon enough."

Crawling on my hands and knees to his side of the sheet, I climbed into his lap and kissed him. "How did I get so lucky?"

Kasper tucked a stray lock of hair behind my ear. "I think I'm the one who should be saying that."

I shook my head. "No way. It's definitely me."

"Agree to disagree?" he asked.

"Nope. I'm a prostitute and you're sort of a saint. I'm right on this one."

Bemused, he said, "I don't think a saint would fall in love with a prostitute, even if she was as adorable as you are right now."

I smiled and squealed inwardly before shrugging and saying, "I don't know. It could happen."

"Maybe," he admitted grudgingly. "But I know for sure a saint wouldn't be thinking of the things I'm thinking of right now."

I raised my brows. "Color me intrigued."

Looking a little chagrined, he reached under his side of the sheet and pulled out two sheets of paper and two pens. "I thought we could do a little compatibility test."

"A compatibility test?" I questioned.

"Yeah, I want to know what a 'lady of the night' likes when she's not trying to please someone else, and I thought you might want a cheat sheet on me since I didn't get to fill out any of the paperwork besides the one for the blood tests."

I laughed. "Oh. *That* kind of compatibility test."

"What do you think? Bad idea?"

"No way!" I said, excited for the chance to see what turned him on. "Give me that pen. I want to know what I'm dealing with."

While we went to work on our respective papers, I wondered what he'd write. Would he have a kink or be vanilla? Would he want something completely at odds with what I favored? Would his answers completely turn me off? With our red-hot chemistry, I hadn't really thought of us being incompatible as a possibility.

Peeking over at his paper, I tried to see what he was scribbling out without being obvious.

"No peeking!" he admonished, turning his paper over. "You can wait until I'm done."

"I think we've established that I'm not very good at waiting," I retorted.

"I have faith in you."

"At least one of us does," I muttered, sulking a bit.

He waved me away with a hand. "Just fill out the form, brat."

I sighed. "Fine."

After another minute, he looked up from his paper to find me watching him expectantly. "Ready to switch?"

"Yes!" I said, bouncing on my knees. "Gimme!"

He laughed. "I hope my answers are worth all of this excitement."

"I think I can work with whatever you put down."

"Ah, that's right. I'm dealing with a professional."

"Damn right," I said, grinning as we traded.

The questions I'd chosen for my clients ran the gamut from their preferred place to cum to what kinks they were into, but I found that even without them being super specific with their answers, I could figure out what most of their tastes were. I just supplemented my own ingenuity when I needed to, and so far, that seemed to work out beautifully. I hadn't had many complaints, and the complaints I did have were usually from nitpicky men who didn't really know what turned them on anyway. Somehow, I didn't think Kasper would be one of those types. He seemed pretty sure of himself.

Kasper looked up from my answers, his mouth quirked in a half smile. "So, you like men to cum inside of you?"

I gave him a sultry smile. "No, I'd like *you* to come inside of me. I haven't forgotten what you said when you were masturbating, you know."

His smile ratcheted up a bit. "Neither have I."

I glanced at the next question. "So, no roleplaying?"

Kasper shrugged. "It's not out of the question, but it's not a real fantasy of mine or anything. That said, if you want to dress up or play strangers in a bar or something, I'm down for it."

"You're making this too easy," I told him.

"Is it supposed to be hard?" he asked.

I wriggled my eyebrows. "In an ideal situation, oh yeah."

He shook his head while reading the next question. "You're a bad girl ... who apparently likes to be tied up."

"I could think of worse things."

"Such as?"

"Not being spanked while I'm tied up?" I suggested.

"I don't think that will be an issue. I have no problem with giving you a little punishment as long as you deserve it."

"Are you saying I have to be bad to get spanked?" I asked, crawling over to sit in his lap again.

He groaned as I shifted my hips. "I'm not sure you won't get spanked before we finish this survey."

"Promises, promises," I purred, beginning a slow rhythm that had me biting my lip as the friction built.

"Are you trying to distract me with this little lap dance routine?" Kasper asked, grabbing my ass and pulling me tight against his erection. "Because if you check my answer to question number five, you'll see that I like to be the dominant one."

"Then it's a good thing I'm naturally submissive, or we'd have to fight it out to be the one on top," I replied, nipping at his lips.

"You on top seems to be working pretty well for me right now." He let his lips trail down my neck before biting me lightly. "Although, if you keep moving those hips the way you are, this sexy survey might have to wait."

"But we're almost to the oral portion of the exam," I said, grinning cheekily.

"I saw you when you were roleplaying with Roger. I know you want my cock in your mouth."

"Correction, I want your cock anywhere you'll put it, Mr. Johansson."

His brows raised in surprise. "Anywhere, Miss Locke?"

"Within reason," I amended. "Don't forget … you're hung like a horse."

"I think that's a bit of an exaggeration."

I held up two fingers measuring a little. "Maybe a teeny bit."

He laughed. "So, where does that leave us?"

"The masturbation question?" I supplied.

"Well, judging by the fact that you're pretty much masturbating both of us right now, I'd say we're both good on that front. More than good if you keep this pace up."

I gave him a wicked grin. "Just try to stop me."

CHAPTER SIXTEEN

A chipper Kasper unlocked the door for me before I could use my key when I arrived the next morning. "Hey," I told him, giving him a quick peck on the lips. "Have you been here long?"

He gave me an appreciative once-over that made me shiver down to my toes. "Not at all. How was your night?"

"Lonely." I smiled ruefully. Kasper knew full well he'd left me a panting ball of sexual desire last night. After our 'masturbation' session, he'd dropped me off at my house, only to pull back into the drive to jump out and lay a kiss on me so hot it might have left scorch marks on the porch.

Grinning, he helped me out of my coat. "There's a fresh pot of coffee in the break room. I thought you might need it."

"You're unbelievably awesome," I said, standing on my tiptoes to give him a better, more thorough kiss. "I mean, really top-notch boyfriend material."

Wrapping his arms around me, he pulled me close. "Right back at you, pretty lady."

I raised my eyebrows in surprise. "You think I'm boyfriend material?"

He shook his head, feigning a very put-upon expression. "You know what I meant, funny girl."

I laughed, eyeing his gorgeous backside as he walked to the rack to hang up my coat. "You know, I've been thinking that we should spend some time together, Kasper, time that's not in this building."

He joined me at the coffeepot and rested his hands on my waist from behind. "How about you come over to my house tonight?"

I turned around in his arms. "How about you make me come at your house tonight?"

Kasper barked out a laugh and lowered his hands to my ass. "How about I make you come right now?"

My heart skipped a few beats as I realized what he was alluding to. "What? Here? Now?"

He shrugged. "Well, why not? We have a little over an hour before Arthur gets here. What do you say to a little foreplay to make you wet for Mr. Evans? You can call it 'prep'."

"Can I make you come, too?" I asked, letting my hands wander toward his belt buckle.

He kissed me long and hard, his hands rubbing slow, sensual circles on my lower back. "If we have time."

"Come on." Grabbing his hand, I pulled him toward the bedroom set up for Shawn in a couple of days. "We can make time."

Kasper laughed and let me drag him to the door before he scooped me up and carried me bride-style into the bedroom. "Okay, but ladies first."

"I have zero problems with that," I told him as he sat me down on my feet. "None, whatsoever."

"Good," he said, retaking my mouth—this time, in an all-out assault. He kissed me deeply, thrusting his tongue inside the moment he ripped my shirt open and backed me onto the bed.

I gasped in surprise at his urgency and groaned into his mouth as he palmed my breasts and pinched the nipples through the fabric. If this was any indication of what was to come, I couldn't wait for what he'd do next.

I didn't have to wait long. With a tug, Kasper pulled my skirt and panties over my hips and threw them across the room. Then he unhooked my bra and slid the ripped shirt over my head, rendering me completely naked.

Kasper sat up on his knees to examine what he'd uncovered. "Fuck," he moaned, disbelief peppering his voice.

Ignoring the compliment, I unbuckled his belt and unbuttoned his jeans, my breath catching when his cock sprang out hard and huge in my hands. I chuckled as I stroked him from base to tip. "Oh, I am going to enjoy this."

Teeth clenched, he growled and stilled my hands. "Not right now, you aren't."

I pouted. "Are you sure?"

"Positive," he said, pulling off his shirt to finally reveal the impressive muscled chest and abs I knew he'd been hiding.

My heart thumped loudly in my ears as he knelt and pulled me to the edge of the mattress. "Kasp—"

And that's when my cell phone rang.

"Don't stop," I begged. "Whoever it is will leave a message."

Kasper shook his head. "Jasmine, it could be Mr. Evans. You need to answer it."

"Fine," I griped, sitting up and grabbing the phone. "But don't you dare move. We're not done here."

He grinned and said, "No, we are not."

I groaned and threw my head back, nearly dropping the phone on my face as I swiped. "H-hello?"

"Jasmine, it's Arthur."

"Hi, Arthur. Are you running late?"

"I'm afraid I'm going to have to cancel tonight's appointment. My flight from Salt Lake City was canceled."

"It's a pity," I purred. "I was in the process of getting ready for you when you called."

"That is a pity," he said in a low voice. "Are you wet for me?"

I moaned softly. "I'm so wet, Arthur."

He groaned. "Make me an appointment next week as soon as you can fit me in, and I'll send something in the way of an apology over in a minute."

"I'll do that. Thank you."

"You're welcome. Oh, and, Jasmine?"

"Yes," I asked breathlessly.

"Come hard for me."

"Yes, sir."

"See you next week, Jasmine."

"See you then, Arthur." I hit end and threw the phone onto the bed. "He's not coming."

"No?" Kasper shot me a mischievous grin. "Then neither are you. At least, not until I get you in my bed," he amended, when he saw my pout. Picking up the torn shirt he'd discarded when undressing me, he frowned. "You'll need to put a robe on. I sort of owe you a shirt."

***

After we made up the room we'd almost defiled for the next client, Kasper drove us to his house. Until now, I hadn't realized just how close I lived to him. He wasn't in the same neighborhood and wasn't as close to me as his parents, but it was a near thing.

"Your house is adorably cute," I remarked, getting out of the truck before he could run over to open my door.

"Thanks?" he replied, staring at his house as if he was trying to figure out what would make me call it cute.

I grinned at his perplexed expression. "You're welcome. And if you're wondering … it's the roses and trellises."

"Ah, that was my mom's doing. She says a home is not a home without a rose garden."

I nodded. "I agree with that, wholeheartedly."

"But you don't have roses at your house."

My eyebrows winged up. "Don't I?"

"Not that I've seen."

"Have you seen my backyard?"

He grinned sheepishly. "No, I have not."

"Then don't you feel silly," I said prissily.

"I guess I do now," he said, trying not to laugh at my sassy attitude. "So, you approve of the house?"

"Kind of hard to do without seeing the inside first."

After unlocking the front door, he swung it wide for me. "Then, be my guest. But be gentle."

I walked in and stopped, marveling at the meticulously clean beigeness of it all. "What in the world?"

"It was painted and furnished when I moved in," he said, taking my coat.

"How long have you lived here?" I asked, walking down the hallway to peek into his bedroom.

"No comment."

"No changes, though?" I shook my head. "Oh, no. You're one of those consummate bachelor types, huh?"

"No, I'm just one of those guys that don't want my mom to decorate for me. Besides, with you here in that bathrobe, who needs decor?"

"Do you like it?" I asked, preening a bit. "It's not too much?"

Placing his hands on my waist, Kasper pulled me closer. "I like it. I'll have to rip your clothes off more often."

Heat bloomed throughout my body, a fire burning me from the inside out. "What specifically do you like about it?" I asked, locking my wrists behind his neck.

"I like the woman wearing it," he said, nipping at my lips.

"Do you now?"

He caressed the bow that would open the robe and gave it a little tug. "Right now, I like how easy it would be to come off. What are you wearing under this? Inquiring minds want to know."

I reached down and plucked the button loose on his jeans. "What are you wearing under these?"

He shuddered as my hand brushed his erection. "Jasmine …" he warned.

I drew my gaze up to his face. His head was down, his eyes were closed, and his jaw was clenched tight. "Do you want to take it slowly?" I asked.

"No," he said, his breath hot against my cheek. "I want you naked and underneath me."

"Bedroom, then?"

His eyes were strikingly blue as he lifted his lids and said, "Yes."

I stepped out of his grasp to make my way to his bedroom, shedding the robe as I went. Glancing back over my shoulder, I found him stock still, staring at me in awe. "Coming?"

"Momentarily, I'm sure."

I gave him a sultry smile and crooked my finger. "Come on, big boy."

CHAPTER SEVENTEEN

Kasper gave me just enough time to get completely undressed before he joined me in the bedroom, naked and as hard as steel.

I stared at his erection and let out a shallow breath. "You know, I'm sort of torn between being terrified of that thing and wanting it twenty-four seven."

He smirked. "I could maybe do two-hundred and forty-seven seconds. I don't think I can last longer than that."

Meeting his gaze, I said, "I don't care how long it is. I just want you inside of me."

Groaning, he nearly tackled me, lifting me so fast, I instinctively wrapped my legs around him. "Hold on to me," he instructed, his deep voice sounding almost frantic.

I did as he asked and was deposited on the bed with Kasper's cock pressed firmly against my center. He rocked against me, teasing my opening as he thrust his tongue in my mouth. Arching against his hardness, I pleaded with my body for him to fill me up as he bit and nipped at my lips. He obliged, reaching between to position himself against my entrance and pushing in so fast and hard, I yelped into his mouth.

"Are you okay?" he asked, his voice full of concern as he looked me over.

"Perfectly so." I ground my hips against him. "But I'm going to need you to move, or I'm going to have to become the dominant in this relationship."

"Fuck," he said through gritted teeth. "You're so fucking tight."

"And yet, you're still not moving," I reminded him, smiling sweetly.

"Give me a moment," he panted. "It's been a while."

"You could always—"

"Don't even say it!" he exclaimed.

I laughed and tightened around him, making him gasp.

"Jasmine," he admonished. "This will be over before it starts if you keep that up."

"Hey, I can do this as many times as it takes. No sweat off my brow."

"No sweat off your brow, eh?" he asked, hitching my legs over his shoulders and snapping his hips.

Normally, I'd have a saucy comeback, but I couldn't respond. I couldn't even think. I was so lost in the delicious pleasure-pain of my body adjusting to his more than adequate size, the sound of his breath, and the spicy sweet smell of his cologne. He was everything at the moment, and I wanted … no, needed more of him.

"What? No more sass?" he taunted, circling his thumb over my hardened clit as he pumped into me. "Nothing else smartass to say?"

I moaned loudly, my body tensing as the first sensations of an orgasm coiled up within me.

"I'll take that as a no." Grinning wickedly, he withdrew and plunged into me hard enough to make me cry out, before beginning a punishing pace that soon had me clutching the comforter underneath me and screaming out his name.

My screams of pleasure seemed to awaken something primal in him. Growling, he sank his fingers into my hair, crushing his mouth to mine in a brutal, bruising kiss and driving his cock into me mercilessly until he roared out his own release, spilling deep inside of me.

Spent, Kasper rested his head on my shoulder as he panted. I ran a hand through his thick, blond hair, acutely aware that he was still hard inside of me. It seemed he would be making good on his promise of filling me up and then fucking me again as soon as he caught his breath.

"Are you okay?" I asked, a silly smile playing at my lips.

He grinned against my neck. "Okay seems like it might be an understatement."

I laughed, knowing exactly how he felt. "All right, then. Penny for your thoughts?"

Raising his head, he braced himself on one elbow and stroked my cheek. "I'm in love with you, Jasmine."

Eyes wide, I asked, "Is this the afterglow talking, or are you serious?"

He chuckled. "A little bit of both, I think. Does that scare you?"

I shook my head. "Not a bit because I'm stupid in love with you, too."

"Stupid in love?" he asked, looking pleased.

"Yes, stupid." I sighed. "I can't stop thinking about you, Kasper. It's distracting as hell."

"Are you sure that isn't because I've got my dick in you right now? I mean, as far as distractions go, having a big cock in you has to be pretty up there."

"I'm sure, but if you want to remind me how distracting it can be, I'm up for it."

"How can I say no to a request like that?" he asked.

"I don't think you can." I hooked a leg around him to force him on his back. "I think you're sort of at my mercy."

"I'm not complaining," he said, groaning as I planted my palms on his chest and began a slow but deliberate rhythm.

"You better not, or I'm charging you for this."

Kasper gave me a devious smile and cupped my breasts, pinching my nipples between unyielding fingers until I gasped. "Do you need to be punished, Jasmine?"

"Yes!" I cried out, reveling in the exquisite pleasure-pain he was giving me. "Harder!"

"If you want it harder, you'll have to earn it," he teased, rolling my aching nipples between his fingers. "Fuck my cock. Show me how much you want it."

I bit my lip and sped up my pace, desperate for the orgasm that I was barreling toward. "Fuck, your cock is so big, so good."

"Touch yourself," he said, squeezing harder. "Come on this big fucking cock."

Without missing a beat, I reached between my legs and rubbed my slick, swollen clit. "Fuck!" I screamed, riding him hard as I worked myself. "I'm going to come. Come with me, Kasper. Fill me up."

No sooner than the words left my mouth, my orgasm hit me like a two-by-four. Writhing in pleasure, I rode him hard, taking every inch he gave me as he yelled out his own completion, then I collapsed onto his chest, hoarse and panting for breath.

"We are never leaving this bed," I said. "Never."

His laugh rumbled in my ear. "We have to. Mr. Harrington is scheduled for tomorrow."

"Nooooo," I whined. "I'm calling in sick."

"Come on, Jasmine," he said, smacking my ass. "Shower time. You go get the water warmed up and I'll grab your robe."

"Are you sure?" I asked, rotating my hips. He was surprisingly hard for someone who had just had back-to-back orgasms.

"Positive, baby. But if I need to bribe you to get off my cock, ice cream could be arranged. I know you have an indecent fascination with lemon custard."

I perked up. "You have lemon custard?"

He smirked at my excitement. "I do. Tempted?"

I kissed him and grudgingly dismounted. "Just so you know, ice cream is probably the only way you would have been able to get me off your dick."

"It's lucky I listen to what you desire then, isn't it?"

Leaning down, I kissed him. "You have everything I desire."

***

Kasper's smile was a promise of sin and debauchery as he looked me over through the glass of the shower. "Need a hand with anything in there?"

I answered his question with a question. "Is there something you'd like to help me with?

He opened the door and stepped into the shower. "There are a whole host of things I'd like to help you with, Jasmine."

"Is that right?"

"Oh, yeah," he said, backing me into the cold tile wall. "A whole host of things."

"What would you start with?" I asked, shivering.

"Your feet."

I laughed. "My feet?"

Kasper grabbed a pouf, poured a dollop of body wash on it, and knelt in front in front of me. "Yep. These tiny, dainty feet."

I couldn't stop the giggle that escaped my lips as he picked up my right foot and slowly ran the soapy pouf across the top of it. "Kasper, I'm ticklish!" I squealed.

"Are you now?" A mischievous grin spread across his face. "Well, that has many possibilities."

I snatched my foot from his grasp. "No, it doesn't!"

Laughing, he stood, relinquishing the pouf when I imperiously held out my hand. "So, no tickling. Got it. Anything else I need to know about?"

"Yes," I told him, wrapping a hand around the thick, hard length in front of me. "Don't trust me to keep my hands to myself when you're naked."

103

"Fuck!" he yelled, falling forward to brace his hands on the wall on either side of me.

I gave him a 'come fuck me' smile and loosened my hold on his cock a little. "Is that an invitation, Mr. Johansson?"

He slid forward between my slick fingers and groaned. "I'm pretty sure I'd give you whatever you asked for right about now."

I squeezed the lather from the pouf onto his cock, tossed it to the shelf beside me, and added my other hand to the mix without missing a beat. "Anything?"

"Anything," he groaned, leaning his forehead against mine as he slowly fucked my soaped-up hands. "Anything you want."

"Good," I purred. "I want to see you come, Kasper."

As if on command, his erection seemed to grow even larger and harder between my palms. "Keep your hands just like they are," he told me, "and you'll get what you ask for in about thirty seconds."

I gave him a throaty little laugh. "Thirty? I think we can do better than that."

"I have no doubt," he said, kissing me. "But I warn you, turnabout is fair play."

I nipped his bottom lip. "Oh, I hope so. Now come for me."

Groaning, he claimed my mouth and pumped once, twice, and then came hard, covering my breasts and stomach before his knees went weak and he had to sit on the tiled corner bench. "Fuck, Jasmine," he gasped out, trying to catch his breath. "Am I even going to survive a relationship with you?"

I stared at his tall, muscled physique and handsome face with what I knew was a wistful, hungry expression. "Even I'm not sure of that, Kasper."

CHAPTER EIGHTEEN

I started drinking at eleven in the morning in preparation of Mr. Harrington's arrival. Though I didn't have to actually drink for him to enjoy it, he always gave me a little something extra if I was actually drunk when he made his visits. I didn't mind at all. In fact, it made it easier to be completely still while he had his way with my body.

Kasper, however, didn't like it.

"Shouldn't you be keeping a clear head?" he asked, watching me make my fourth double rum and Coke of the day.

"Maybe if I didn't have you here to watch over me. But since you are, I don't mind imbibing. Besides, he paid me an extra five thousand the last time I got smashed."

"That's sort of creepy."

I shrugged. "I don't know why he prefers it this way, but there doesn't seem to be any nefarious reasons behind it or anything. Judging by his email responses, I think he may just be shy about what turns him on."

Kasper nodded, but his expression didn't change. "How long before he comes?"

I checked the clock. "Ten minutes." I grabbed the bottle and my glass. "I have to get in there. See you in thirty or so?"

"I'll be here," he grumbled.

I gave him a reassuring smile and walked down the hall to the plainest of the rooms. Tim Harrington wasn't picky about the where, only the how. Like him, I employed the same line of simple thinking. I didn't care where it happened, just that I was getting paid for it.

Dimming the lights on my way in, I set the bottle of rum and my glass on the nightstand and pulled off my clothes until I was down to my skimpy underwear. I usually didn't wear any with Tim, but I'd picked up this set of crotchless panties and a cupless bra just for him. For the thirty thousand dollars he paid me last time, he should get a little something extra.

"Wow," Kasper said through the intercom.

I did a little drunken turn and slurred, "You like 'em?"

"A lot," he responded.

"I have them in red, too. I know you like that color on me."

"I like any color on you, Jasmine."

I grinned at the camera.

"Incoming," he said. "Mr. Harrington is at the lobby door."

"Shit!" I exclaimed, scrambling onto the bed. I laid on my back with a leg cocked up and said, "Buzz him in."

I heard the buzzer sound and the echo of fast footsteps outside the bedroom door before the knob turned and Tim Harrington stepped inside. Moving slowly, he was as quiet as a mouse as he took off his clothes and put them on the bedside chair. I knew this was so that he wouldn't "wake" me. Tim was as good of an actor as I was when it came down to it. He liked to be in his own little fantasy.

I felt a soft hand trace up my leg from my ankle to thigh and heard his breathing speed up as he neared my center. I knew he would be touching himself while he was touching me. He always masturbated while he decided what he wanted to do first.

"So beautiful," he whispered, climbing onto the bed to rub the head of his cock against my wetness. "I could come without even being inside of you."

At an achingly slow pace, he positioned himself at my core and slid inside, barely moving once he was in. It was obvious he was trying not to come yet and having a hard time of it. I kept still, my face immobile as he struggled. Finally, after a few slow strokes, he came inside of me. I could feel cum dripping down my ass as he stroked his semi-erect dick along the slit and pushed back inside to fuck me again.

This was pretty typical of him. In his past visits, he would come three or four times before he tired out, sometimes easing me onto my stomach to fuck me from behind, sometimes dipping my mouth open with his thumb and slowly filling my mouth with his cock as far as he could before ejaculating on my face and tits.

The only constants of my time with Tim was that I would be covered with his cum before he left, and I would be paid handsomely for it. Even without the booze, that would've been fine by me. Tim Harrison wanted me, and he wasn't ashamed to use me in the way he needed. That turned me on. I liked a man who was honest about what he needed to get off, and honestly, for what he paid me, I would do close to anything to make him come back for more.

With a low whispered oath, Mr. Harrington pulled his cock out and replaced it with two testing fingers before circling my clit with his thumb. I sighed as if heavy with sleep as he fingered me and turned my head toward the edge of the bed, leaving my mouth conveniently ajar.

Seizing the opportunity, Tim climbed off the bed to push his dick between my parted lips and began to gently fuck my mouth. Groaning softly, he came almost immediately, filling my mouth until it spilled out onto my cheek and the pillow underneath.

Just as expected, he didn't stop the minute movements he was making. He only continued to pump himself into my mouth before finally deciding to maneuver me to my side and wedge a pillow behind my back. Pushing my knee upward, he exposed my dripping wet pussy and bent down to lick my clit.

Surprised, I pretended to sleepily move to readjust the angle and open myself to his machinations. He'd never licked his cum off my body before, but now seemed keen on it, dragging his wide tongue from my clit to my opening then dipping inside to taste what he'd left behind.

"You taste so good," he whispered as he rose up behind me and slid himself home. "I want to cover you with my cum from head to toe."

Fucking me a little harder than before, Tim reached down and rubbed my clit as he leaned forward to take my breast in his mouth, barely using his teeth to nibble on the nipple.

It was all I could do not to come right then and there. The feel of him deep inside of me while he circled my clit and bit my breast was bringing me to the brink of orgasm, no matter how weird his fetish.

"You're so tight and hot," he moaned. "Are you dreaming about this dick sliding in and out of that pussy full of my cum?"

I sighed again, letting the slightest of cries escape from my lips.

"You like that, don't you?" he asked, though he knew I wouldn't respond. "You want me to cum all over you, don't you, you fucking slut?"

In truth, as drunk as I was, I didn't care what he did as long as he kept touching my clit and fucking me the way he was. I was so close to coming apart, I couldn't think of anything but his cock and the pulsing need between my thighs.

Groaning loudly, he doubled down on his efforts, putting everything he had into fucking my boneless body and pinching my soaked clit hard between his slick fingers. "Come for me," he said roughly. "Come on this cock, and I'll give you the cum you want."

I was helpless to obey, and the orgasm struck me hard, nearly making me break my concentration on being motionless as it coursed through me.

"Yes," Tim hissed, pushing my knee up to my chest to fuck me at a brutal pace. "Make that tight pussy come on this hard cock, you fucking whore."

Ignoring the insult, I took every inch he gave me, letting wave after wave of pleasure roll through my body as he quickly brought himself to a final orgasm, pulling his dick out at the last second to come on my ass, tits, and face.

Collapsing on top of me, he chuckled to himself and licked the cum from the side of my breast. "Email me with your availability," he said. "Next week, I'm going to show you how I make women like you scream."

I didn't answer, just laid there, pretending to sleep as he wiped himself down with some tissues, got dressed, and left the room.

A minute after he walked out the door, Kasper said, "He's gone."

I lifted my arm and gave him a thumbs up.

"Need any help?"

I sat up and grimaced at the huge amount of cum covering everything in the vicinity of the bed. "No. And turn the camera off. I don't want you to see me like this."

"Will do, boss."

***

After I showered, I got dressed and met Kasper in the lobby for a ride home, all the while hoping he wouldn't be disgusted by what he'd seen today. Tim was one of my messier clients.

"Hey," he said, greeting me with a smile that didn't reach his eyes.

"Hey."

He handed me my coat. "So, that was Mr. Harrington."

I rolled my eyes as I shrugged it on. "In all his sticky glory."

He chuckled. "Is it normal to have that much semen? I mean, holy shit … that was a lot."

"You tell me. You're the one with the penis."

"Well, if you ask me, there was nothing normal about what just went down in there." He shook his head. "I mean, the guy was creepy as fuck."

"I'll agree with that. Tim has been coming here for three years, but he's never spoken to me like that or … uh, did the things he did tonight. It was odd."

"I don't want to overstep my boundaries, but I think it's time to stop seeing him."

I nodded in agreement. "I hate to lose the money, but yeah, definitely. I just got an email telling me, in graphic detail, how much he enjoyed fucking me and how my orgasm tells him I'm ready for the next level of his fetish."

His eyes widened. "Whoa."

"Yeah. Something's way off with him. The insults and that comment about showing me how he makes women like me scream, that made me a little nervous."

"Nervous isn't the word I would use."

"No? What word would you use?"

"Homicidal, maybe, but definitely not nervous. How much money will you lose if you cut him loose, if you don't mind me asking?"

I sighed. "He paid me twenty-five thousand dollars for today."

His eyes widened. "That's a lot of money, Jasmine."

"It is, but I have other clients. Really, I'm not too heartbroken about it. Dealing with all that semen, it's not pleasant."

Kasper shook his head. "It wasn't pleasant to watch, either."

Sighing, I sat down in a lobby chair. "You know, I never thought I'd say this, but after that, I'm actually looking forward to Mr. Evans tomorrow."

CHAPTER NINTEEN

Kasper was uncharacteristically quiet on the drive to my house. I wasn't quite sure if it was because of our budding relationship or whether it was because of the scary episode with Mr. Harrington, but I knew that whatever it was, he was really upset.

I laid a gentle hand on his thigh. "Do you want to talk about it?"

Kasper pressed his full lips into a thin line and huffed out a breath through his nose before speaking. "I couldn't stand watching him fuck you. I wanted to rip him off your body and throw him outside, clothed or not. I know I said I could handle you sleeping with other guys, but that guy, I just wanted to throttle him."

I nodded. "I get that that client wasn't ideal. He was definitely out of line, but I think this has more to do with you and I being in love than what happened in there, don't you?"

He glanced over at me. "I love you, Jasmine. I don't want to see you hurt or degraded, no matter the amount of money they're willing to pay you."

I leaned over as far as my seatbelt would allow and leaned my head on his shoulder. "I love you, too. We'll figure this out, okay?"

"I know we will," he said, kissing the top of my head. "I just need a few minutes to cool off."

"Are you sure you don't want me to go to your mom and dad's house with you for the barbecue?"

"No, baby. You're tired and look like you're still pretty hammered. You don't have to do that. I've been going to these things by myself since the beginning of time. And besides, there's something I want to talk to them about while I'm there. I'm not sure you'd feel comfortable."

I lifted my head to look at him. "You're not going to chastise your mom for not telling you how she knew about my job, are you?"

He laughed as he turned into my driveway and put the truck into park. "No, she can keep her witchy ways a secret."

"Good," I said, unbuckling my seatbelt. "I like your mom. You be nice to her."

"I'm always nice to her," he scoffed. "I'm a nice guy."

"Says the guy who stole my éclair and ate it."

"Hey, that theft got you to rub your 'lady parts' on me. I regret nothing."

Leaning over the center console, I kissed him. "I like rubbing my 'lady parts' on you. It's one of my favorite activities."

"I knew I should have kissed you that day," he said regrettably.

"What do you mean? You did kiss me that day."

"I mean before Roger came. I should have kissed you when we were tousling over the doughnut."

I shook my head. "I think I like what we did better. If you would've kissed me, we might have fucked earlier, and then I wouldn't have seen you masturbate. That memory gives me something to think about on lonely nights."

"Remind me to masturbate in front of you more often, then," he said, kissing me with a hunger that wasn't there a few moments earlier. "I want you thinking of me when you come."

"Trust me, Kasper. I'm not thinking of anyone else when I come."

"Will you think of me tonight?" he asked, letting his hand rest on my ass.

"Why don't you just come over," I purred. "That way, I won't have to think about you. We can actually do all of those dirty things I like to think about."

It seemed as if he was considering it, but then he shook his head. "No, I'll give you time to yourself tonight. That way you'll have a chance to miss me."

"I already miss you," I said, sticking my bottom lip out.

"You'll survive," he told me, lightly biting my lip.

"Fine. Pick me up tomorrow for Mr. Evan's rescheduled appointment?" I asked. "It's on the Google Calendar."

Kasper ran a thumb over my cheek and placed a tender kiss on my lips. "I'll be there."

***

After I was considerably soberer, I nuked a microwavable meal and got ready for bed. I was hoping that Kasper would call or make a surprise visit, but there had been radio silence since he'd dropped me off this afternoon. I couldn't blame him for needing a bit of space. I'd known seeing me with someone so soon after we'd declared our love for one another was going to make things dicey. I just hoped his mom would set his head on straight while he was there.

I was dozing in and out as I lounged with my favorite giant teddy bear and season four of *Gilmore Girls*, only to be jolted out of bed when I heard my doorbell peal several times in quick succession. A quick glance at my phone told me it was almost midnight. Would Kasper come by this late? Surely his parents' barbecue wouldn't have lasted this long.

Cautiously, I climbed out of bed, grabbed the baseball bat I kept behind the door for emergencies, and tiptoed toward the door. It rang several more times before I asked, "Who's there?"

"It's me," came Kasper's slurred voice. "Will you let me in?"

I unlocked the door and opened it to find a thoroughly intoxicated Kasper. He was leaning on the front of the porch railing to keep himself upright. Waving at the Uber driver who was waiting to see if he needed to take him anywhere else, I said, "Hi."

"Hi," he said, leering at my breasts in my tank top.

Laughing, I wrapped an arm around his waist. "You better get in here."

He stumbled away from the railing, leaning heavily on me. "Okay."

Once he was inside, I closed the door and led him into the bedroom. "Have a little too much to drink tonight?" I asked, lowering him onto my bed.

He held up his thumb and forefinger, measuring a little bit. "Just a few beers … and shots."

Surprised, I raised my brows as I unlaced his boots and tugged them off. "Wild night at your parents?"

"No, Uncle David had a card game after the barbecue."

"I see. And is he as drunk as you are?"

He raised his head, and for the first time, I noticed the black eye he was sporting. "Fuck him."

"What happened, Kasper?" I asked, pushing back his hair. "Did you two get into a fight?"

"He just wouldn't shut up about you being a prostitute," he replied angrily. "He said not to fall in love with you because when someone came along with money in the bank, you'd fuck him and forget all about me. He said you'd fuck anyone with a dick. So, I decked him."

I ground my teeth together, wanting to drive to his house to deck him myself. "Well, I appreciate you defending my honor, Kasper, but I don't like to see you hurt."

"I'm not hurt."

"That shiner says otherwise," I told him. "Do want ice or a raw steak or something?"

"No, I just need you."

Kasper reached out to pull me into his lap, but fell over, causing me to fall on the bed beside him. I laughed as he wrapped his arms around my waist and buried his face into my ponytail.

"I love you," he slurred. "I love you so damn much."

"And I love you," I told him, glad he seemed to be calmer now. "Do you want to get undressed so we can go to bed?"

"In a minute." He slid his left hand from my waist to the edge of my boy shorts.

My breath caught as he dipped his hand under the band, into my panties. "Kasper—"

"Shhh," he interrupted.

I closed my eyes and moaned as he rubbed slow circles over my clit, forgetting everything that I was about to say.

"Did you think about me fucking this pussy tonight?" he growled into my ear.

"I only think about your cock in this pussy, Kasper," I told him. In truth, I had been so tired when I got home, I hadn't thought of anything but collapsing in bed, but I knew that wasn't what he wanted to hear. Right now, he wanted to be soothed. And if this was the way he wanted to go about that, I was all for it.

"Did you come thinking about my fat cock filling up this tight, wet pussy?"

"Yes," I groaned, grabbing his hip and digging my nails into him when he slipped his right hand into my panties and drove two long fingers inside of me, never stopping the slow, insistent circles on my clit.

"Come again," he demanded, fucking me rough and hard with his fingers. "I want you soaking wet for me, Jasmine. I want to feel you come for me. Come!"

As soon as the order fell from his lips, I came instantly, screaming out my completion and bucking on his fingers until I couldn't make myself move anymore.

When he felt my tense body relax, exhausted and sated, Kasper chuckled and gently removed his hands. "I nearly came when you screamed," he whispered. "You're so fucking sexy."

Smiling, I turned over in his arms to kiss him. "I can take care of that with my mouth if you'd like."

He returned my smile with his own contented one and pulled me closer to rest his head against mine. "Later, baby. When there's not two of you and the room's not spinning."

CHAPTER TWENTY

I woke up with the afternoon sun shining brightly into my bedroom window and a gentle hand kneading my breast, which was a sharp contrast to the hard dick pressing into my ass. I grinned. "Good morning, Kasper."

"Morning," he rumbled. "Care for a little cock?"

"Why? Do you know someone with a little cock?" I asked cheekily.

He groaned. "It's too early for sass."

I turned over in his arms and propped my head up on an elbow. "It's never too early for sass. Besides, I don't have time for dick, small or not. Mr. Evans is coming in at three."

"Is he asking for his usual?"

"Do you really want to know," I asked, slipping my hand around his erection.

"No," he replied, giving me a hungry look. "What I want is to feel you on my cock. After grinding on your ass, trying to wake you up, I'm not going to last long anyway."

I laughed sultrily as I pulled off my panties and straddled his hips, sliding my wetness along his length in a slow, sensual lap dance-style rhythm before kissing my way down his stomach and taking what I could of him into my mouth.

Groaning loudly, Kasper bunched my sloppy ponytail in his hands and pumped his hips, fucking my mouth fast and hard. "Touch yourself while I fuck your pretty mouth, Jasmine. I want you wet for Arthur's cock."

He didn't have to ask me twice. I reached between my legs and began to furiously rub my clit to please him. Nothing turned me on more than obeying Kasper in the bedroom. For him, I didn't mind relinquishing control. For him, I would do anything.

"Fuck, you look good with my cock in your mouth," Kasper said through clenched teeth, and with a sudden roar, he gripped my hair painfully tight. I whimpered, the pain thrusting me into climax as he shot load after load of his own orgasm down my throat.

Collapsing back onto the pillows, he let go of my hair and panted as he watched me wipe my mouth on the back of my hand and climb up to join him.

"Maybe Mr. Evans will cancel again today," he said hopefully.

I chuckled and kissed his nipple. "Fuck, I hope so. I can't seem to go more than twelve hours without your dick somewhere inside of me."

"Trust me, Jasmine. I'm not complaining."

***

Forty minutes after Kasper reluctantly left to go home to take a quick shower and change, there was a knock at my front door. "That was a quick hour," I called, laughing as the door swung open to reveal Kasper's bruised and battered uncle, David Lanka.

"Hey, David," I said, dumbfounded as to how he knew where I lived. "Is everything okay? Is something wrong with Lukas and Annika?"

His smile was bright, but it didn't reach his eyes. "Not at all. I just dropped by to see if you were up for riding on a better cock than Kasper's."

"W-what?" I stammered.

He smirked. "Come on, Jasmine. You're a whore. You know how this thing works."

I could feel my cheeks burning as my anger rose. "I'm sorry, David, but that's not going to be possible … ever."

Affronted, he asked, "And why not? You're fucking Kasper. You fuck a lot of guys from what you told us."

Gritting my teeth, I took a deep breath before I answered. "David, Kasper is my boyfriend. And yes, I do 'fuck a lot of guys',

118

but those guys are carefully selected clients, and they pay me very well to perform for them. Prostitution isn't something I do for kicks. It's a job, just like anyone else's job."

"Okay," he said, his fake smile ratcheting up as he played along with what he clearly thought was some little game of mine. "How much do you charge for your 'job'? I'm sure I can pay whatever your rate is."

"I start at fifteen thousand," I told him, making my voice as cold and businesslike as I could. "And there are health inquiries and background checks that must be done a week in advance before I schedule the actual sex. But like I already told you, that won't be happening. I don't feel comfortable having sex with someone Kasper views as family, and I don't think he'd be comfortable with it, either."

"Bullshit!" he said, becoming visibly angry.

Shaken, I took a step back inside. It was a dumb decision on my part—giving him the opportunity to squeeze past me into my living room—one that I would berate myself for repeatedly when I got away from him, but I wasn't thinking straight. I had been frightened of David's abrupt change in demeanor and just wanted to put distance between us.

"I didn't invite you in," I said, bristling when he moved into my personal space. "You need to leave."

He grabbed my arm and squeezed it painfully. "Oh, I think we both know that's not going to happen."

"Let go of me!" I yelled, snatching my arm out of his grasp and pushing him toward the open door.

David's cruel laugh made a shiver run down my spine. "Jasmine, don't be stupid!" he hissed, yanking me closer. "Just take my money and give me what I want!"

"The lady said, 'no'," a cold, calm voice said from the doorway.

At the sound of Kasper's voice, David nearly shoved me away in an attempt to look innocent. I stumbled but sighed audibly in relief. Kasper had done what he promised when I hired him. He had kept me safe.

"Hey, man—" David began, but Kasper cut him off.

"You're a married man, David. What are you doing here trying to fuck my girlfriend instead of your wife? She's already forgiven you so many times I can't even count. How could you?"

David laughed and gave him a practiced, good-natured smile that probably had charmed many a person into thinking he wasn't a total douchebag in the past. "Look, Kasper. She's just a whore, and I'm a man with more needs than my wife can handle. There's no need for anyone to know about this."

"There's every need for her to know what a slimy piece of adulterous shit you are," Kasper retorted as he made his way to me. "Are you okay, baby?"

"Baby?" David scoffed. "Are you kidding me? She's a fucking whore. She wouldn't be fucking you if you weren't paying her."

"Kasper pays me nothing," I seethed, barely keeping my urge to throttle him under control. "I fuck him whenever and wherever he wants. He deserves this pussy. You, on the other hand, have two seconds to get the fuck out of this house before I give you worse than Kasper gave you last night."

Kasper smiled nastily at his uncle. "You heard the lady. Get the fuck out and don't ever come back."

"You're a fool," David spat. "You mark my words. She will never change. She'll always spread her legs for money. That's what whores do."

Fed up, I broke away from Kasper and kicked David square in the chest. With a yelp, he flew through the opened doorway and landed on his ass on the porch. I strode toward him, ready to kick him again, and he scrambled back in fear. Shaking my head at how pathetic he was, I slammed the door and locked it behind me before tears started streaming down my face.

"Baby, don't cry," Kasper said, wrapping me in his arms and hugging me tight. "He's not worth it."

"I know," I whispered, nodding. "I'm just not sure what I would've done if you hadn't shown up. How did you know he was here?"

Kasper smiled and wiped the tears from my cheeks with his thumbs. "I had no idea he was here. I just couldn't wait to see you again. I've been dying to ask you something since I left my parent's house last night."

I pulled back from him. "Ask me what? What's going on?"

He shoved a hand into his right jeans pocket, pulled out a red velvet box, and got down one knee. "Will you marry me, Jasmine?"

I stared at him, openmouthed. "What?"

Grinning, he opened the box to show me a vintage square-cut emerald ring just a shade darker than my eyes. "I love you, Jasmine. I want you to be my wife."

Stunned, I stammered, "Y-you … you're f-fired, Kasper."

His smile fell. "What? I don't understand."

"You're fired," I reiterated.

Flustered, he stood up. "But why, Jasmine? You have to have someone protecting you while you do your job."

I shrugged. "Not anymore. I quit."

"You quit?" he asked warily.

"Yeah, I can't be a married woman and a prostitute. That's just unseemly."

Forehead furrowed, he asked, "So, you'll marry me?"

I laughed. "Yes!"

Kasper whooped for joy then grabbed me, kissing me long and hard. When he finally let me come up for air, he said, "I love you so fucking much, Jasmine, but this is going to change your life. Are you sure I'm worth it?"

I smiled up at my tall, strong Viking of a man. "Totally worth it. And besides, I'm filthy rich. I've been charging ten to forty thousand dollars a client for five years. We may have to find other jobs, but we'll be millionaires while we do it."

Kasper shook his head in disbelief. "You're amazing."

"You better believe it," I told him, standing on the tips of my toes for another kiss. "Now put that ring on my finger and get me to the office. We have just enough time for you to get me wet for Mr. Evans."

"One more for old time's sake?" he asked, chuckling at my sass.

I winked at him as he slid the ring on my finger. "From now on, you can be the one to pay me to do whatever you like."

Kasper cupped my face in his hands and kissed me gently. "Baby, you've got a customer for life."

THE END

Also by J.D. Nelson

<u>Wicked Ways Series</u>

A Night of Wickedness
All I Want For Christmas Are My Two Front Fangs: A Wicked
Ways Companion Novel
Wolves Will Be Wolves
Too Cute To Spook: A Wicked Ways Companion Novel

<u>Night Aberrations Series</u>

Night Aberrations
The Fire within the Night

<u>Havenwood Falls Sin & Silk</u>

Plans Laid Bare
Soul Laid Bare

About the Author

JD Nelson is a Bestselling Author of Fantasy Romance and Adult Paranormal Romance. An avid time-waster, JD enjoys watching TV and listening to audiobooks when she really should be writing. JD loves to hear from her readers. You can contact her through her website, AuthorJDNelson.com, or on Facebook, where she spends an alarming amount of time chatting with her many Author and reader friends, much to the dismay of her continually neglected manuscripts.

JD Nelson's Facebook
www.facebook.com/NightAberrations
JD Nelson's Twitter
https://twitter.com/authorjdnelson
JD Nelson's Facebook Fan Page
www.facebook.com/JDNelsonsNightAberrations
JD Nelson's Fan Club
http://www.facebook.com/groups/269730583130725/